ENCOUNTER WITH KIRAN

ALSO BY NAYANTARA SAHGAL

Fiction

A Time to be Happy (1958)
This Time of Morning (1962)
Storm in Chandigarh (1969)
The Day in Shadow (1971–72)
A Situation in New Delhi (1977)
Rich Like Us (1985)
Plans For Departure (1986)
Mistaken Identity (1988)
Lesser Breeds (2003)
Day of Reckoning (Short Stories) (2015)
When the Moon Shines by Day (2017)
The Fate of Butterflies (2018)

Non-Fiction

Prison and Chocolate Cake (1954)
From Fear Set Free (1962)
Point of View (1997)
Before Freedom: Nehru's Letters to His Sister 1909–1947 (Ed., 2000)
Relationship (with E.N. Mangat Rai; 2008)
Jawaharlal Nehru: Civilizing a Savage World (2010)
Indira Gandhi: Tryst With Power (2012)
The Story of India's Freedom Movement (2013)
The Political Imagination (2014)
Nehru's India: Essays on the Maker of a Nation (Ed., 2015)

ENCOUNTER WITH KIRAN

Fragments from a Relationship

Nayantara Sahgal

SPEAKING TIGER

SPEAKING TIGER BOOKS LLP
125A Shahpur Jat, Ground Floor,
New Delhi 110049

First published by Speaking Tiger Books 2021

ISBN: 978-93-5447-193-3
eISBN: 978-93-5447-198-8

10 9 8 7 6 5 4 3 2 1

The article 'A Hindu Speaks' by Nayantara Sahgal on p. 98 was first published in *The Tribune* on 8 October 2017; the letters from Kiran Nagarkar to Prime Minister Narendra Modi (p. 118) and Finance Minister Arun Jaitley (p. 129) were first published in *Scroll.in*, on 29 March 2016 and 9 March 2017 respectively, and have been reproduced here with permission of the publishers.

Typeset in Adobe Garamond Pro by SÜRYA, New Delhi
Printed at Shree Maitrey Printech Pvt. Ltd., Noida

In memory of a comradeship in hard times

Comrades in arms: Nayantara Sahgal (above) and (below) Kiran Nagarkar

Sudharak Olwe

CONTENTS

AUTHOR'S NOTE

Kiran and I were strangers to each other—having met just once before at a literary festival in Delhi in 2002—when he came to Dehradun in 2014 to talk to me about my writing, an interview intended for the Chandigarh Literary Festival's archives. He might have come and gone and that would have been the end of the encounter. Instead, it became a beginning, continuing in an exchange of emails. Emails are not a celebrated form of keeping in touch. They don't have the prestige of letters, but they have an immediacy that letters can't have. Our mails made for the sense of a presence nearby with whom it became natural to share views, feelings and daily doings. It brought two writers into each others' orbit and into an involvement with each others' lives. Writers get to know each other through their work, and we talked about our own and each others' writing in our mails, but without this correspondence—fragments of which appear in *Encounter*—we would not have known each other as persons. All the same, Kiran's novels played a big part in my getting to know the person who wrote them.

If I were to pack them all into one single volume, I would title it 'The Power and the Fury'. I saw his entire oeuvre as a literature of revolt written by a man in revolt, against inequality, poverty, depravity and inhumanity of every kind. It foregrounded the savageries that are inflicted on women and taken for granted in our society and *Jasoda* is an unsparing re-creation of woman as chattel. *Jasoda* and his other novels confront us with this ongoing barbarism in language and scenes that shock. But in other novels solemnity becomes hilarious in the telling. A scene in the *Ravan & Eddie* trilogy shows these two unlikely heroes transporting a dead body down the stairs of Chawl No. 17 in Mumbai's Mazagaon for eventual disposal, and having to manoeuvre the bier with minutest care to prevent the corpse from falling off it at every precarious turn. Ravan and Eddie became my favourite fiction characters. Their home, a teeming tenement that immortalizes the appalling conditions in which thousands live and die, becomes a saga of vigorous survival in these conditions, which is what made the trilogy my most exhilarating read.

Cuckold, the first Nagarkar novel I read, remains in a class by itself. In this fictitious slice of Rajput history, Kiran's own irreverence takes an irreverent swipe at unnecessary wars, needless heroism, and matters considered sacred. As I read it, the story acquired the massive scale and grandeur of architecture. Within this masterful evocation of daunting Rajput traditions, the saint-princess Meerabai, quite undaunted, carries on her passionate love affair with Lord Krishna. Her husband, Maharaj Kumar Bhojraj of Chittor, would have died unknown and unsung but for Kiran's creation of a baffled, intrigued and infuriated cuckold who plays second fiddle to his wife's lover. *Cuckold* prepared me for the fact that there was no question of sitting back and relaxing with a book by Nagarkar, with all that keeps rearing up from the page.

The comic and tragic tangled in his storytelling because they were the jumble called life. But pain figured large in his fiction as a solitary unshareable experience. *Seven Sixes Are Forty-three* is suffused with an atmosphere of aloneness and suffering. Started when he was twenty-five, abandoned and then completed seven years later, it was written in Marathi. Being half Marathi myself, but brought up Kashmiri, I regretted not being able to read *Seven Sixes* in the original, but I read the English translation Kiran sent me and felt it had the poignancy of being closer at the time of writing to his experience of recurring illness in childhood, and to the lost lover who stays absent through the story, yet remains at the heart of it. His emails had acquainted me with the perennial ill health he still coped with and made light of, refusing to let it interfere with his enjoyment of life to the hilt.

I discovered a bond with Kiran apart from writing. Being born political myself, into a family that took part in the fight for freedom from British rule, I found in him a like interest and concern with national and international affairs. But there was a difference. Mine was a natural consequence of my background and upbringing. His had an intensity that came of his own observation and experience of the world around him. His anger at the assault on democratic rights was hammered out in articles and in letters to an uncaring regime. We met at a time of fundamental political change in India. The India we knew was disappearing under a government that had declared war on our age-old civilization of inclusiveness and the secular republic we had built since independence. It was not a time for personal or literary withdrawal and neither of us withdrew from the fray. If Kiran had a political philosophy, it was this: 'If we don't take a stand and make our voices heard against the violation of human rights, brutality, prejudice, hatred and persecution of the powerless, we are squarely responsible for the consequences of our inaction.'

Kiran had once written to me about the deafening noises religion makes. If he had a religion, it was Kabir who appears in *God's Little Soldier* and becomes the subject of *The Arsonist*. Of *Arsonist* he writes: 'This book found itself being written because every now and then the ghastly things that were happening in Kabir's own country, India...compelled me to ask how he would have responded to events that were recurring centuries after his death: the lynchings, the hate campaigns, the loss of humanity, sanity, and compassion...the bottomless greed and mendacity...the ceaseless violence.... Would Kabir have managed to shake us awake and rise?'

Kiran was the part believer, part blasphemer that Kabir was, and above all a lover of life. In *Arsonist* a mulla asks the Weaver, if he had to choose between God and a woman he loved—or for that matter, a song or a sunset—which would he choose? The Weaver chooses the woman, the song and the sunset. God had eternity on his side and could wait. 'Will the woman, the song or the sunset wait for me?'

NAYANTARA SAHGAL

Dehradun, July 2021

PART ONE

Building Bonds

A Correspondence Between Two Writers

It was at a literature festival in Delhi in February 2002 that I met Kiran Nagarkar for the first time. We had been together at another litfest held a few days earlier at Neemrana Fort in Rajasthan, as we later discovered, but our paths hadn't crossed. (The Neemrana festival, called 'At Home and Away', organized by the Indian Council for Cultural Relations, was probably the precursor of the Jaipur Litfest and the plethora of litfests that followed. The event in Delhi was a follow-up to Neemrana, and seemed to have been held mainly for V.S. Naipaul, the visiting Nobel Laureate.)

After meeting Kiran, I bought his novel *Cuckold*, and wrote to him about it on 7 April 2002: 'Dear Kiran, I got back from the Delhi festival, attended to tax returns, and then bought *Cuckold*. *Cuckold* is a triumph. I read it slowly, every word. It is wonderfully engaging all the way through. Putting it into contemporary language gives it a peculiar immediacy—lifts it out of "history" and gives it tremendous force and impact. I could say more—but quite simply, it's a triumph.

'The litfest, in retrospect, seems hollow—dominated by the strange assertion (supported by notable Indians themselves) that there's no writing worth reading except what's written in English. (*Cuckold* makes me curious as to your creativity in Marathi.) There was also no interaction between the mighty Naipaul and Indian language writers. He seemed content to stay cocooned in his own little coterie of admirers.

'By way of return for a great reading experience I'm sending you *Rich Like Us* published in 1985 abroad—but a new paperback was brought out by HarperCollins India a few years ago. I only have copies of the original English edition with me at the moment. I hope very much that you'll enjoy it—a book is a way of getting to know the author better.

'It was lovely meeting you. With all good wishes, Nayantara.

'P.S. I got your address from HarperCollins—and discovered it's the same road where I lived for fourteen years in Bombay, first at Dil Pazir, then at Mafatlal Park.'

After that first meeting I heard that Kiran had ordered some of my books from HarperCollins, the publisher we shared at the time. But we had no further interaction until,. in 2014, I heard from Kiran. On 11 October 2014 he wrote: 'Dear Nayantaraji—I have thought of calling when I have particularly enjoyed reading a passage from one of your books but I am far too unsure of myself and get tongue-tied and am always worried that I will be intruding on your privacy. One of the unexpected pleasures of your work was your sense of humour. I found your introduction to *Prison & Chocolate Cake*[1] not only wise but I also thought you were making an extremely important point when you talked about not disowning one's past. Since like you, I am not into hagiography, I will not glide over the occasional problem I may have with something or the other in your work (for instance the narrator's mother taking off with Yusouf in *Mistaken Identity* at the end which was fun but…) but there was much to learn and enjoy in the little I have read of your work. I will spare you my demented rage with our people for having lost our national narrative which is and should have always been our freedom struggle and its unique ideological basis, and my diatribes against our people for failing to understand that your Mamu[2] and Gandhiji are far more relevant today than ever before. I wish I could have sat with you and listened to you for hours but luckily I stay in Mumbai and will not be allowed to harass you. Warmest regards, Kiran.'

I replied that it would be interesting to meet and talk, and if there was any chance of his visiting Dehradun, he should let me know and come and have a meal.

'Dear Nayantaraji,' he wrote three days later, 'will you please send me your address and any instructions that will make it easy to find your place? I hope I will get time with you just to listen to you on any subject you want to talk about. Would it be okay if I brought along someone to record your views so that they can be archived in a permanent collection at the Chandigarh literary festival archives? Warm regards, Kiran.'

Kiran, it transpired, had suggested to Mitul Dikshit, the founder-director of the Chandigarh Literature Festival, that a recording of me talking about my work should be kept in the festival archives, and that he would like to interview me for this purpose. Mitul had readily agreed and had arranged for Kiran to come to Dehradun along with a team to record the interview.

We had lunch when Kiran and his team arrived, and then—in no way an 'interview'—we talked about my work, mainly my novel *Rich Like Us*. He was intrigued that its main character, Rose, was an

English Cockney and I told him how this had come about. When I had lived in Bombay in the 1960s, among my friends was a couple—an English wife and an Indian husband who was still married to his Indian first wife and had children by her. It was an intriguing situation and my novel took off from it but departed from it in every other way. Creating Rose as a Cockney set her apart from the English ruling class of the time, and accounts for the special qualities of her character.

After this visit, on 31 December, Kiran wrote: 'Dear Nayantaraji, I have been unforgivably remiss in keeping in touch with you though in truth not a day passes when I am not thinking of you. I suspect despite all my cynicism I am an old-fashioned believer in either astral connections or bonds that are beyond the ken of human beings.

'How are you? Very often these days I feel utterly despondent about what is happening to this beloved and benighted country of ours and then I look to you and draw succour from your fortitude and iron will.

'Renuka Chatterjee of Speaking Tiger has been telling me about the book of essays on Nehru[3] that you are editing and that you want me to write for it. I have zero confidence in myself for the simple reason that while I have an emotional and extremely strong bond with Jawaharlalji, I am very conscious of the fact that I am not equipped to write about him. Of course I will give it a try both for what he means to me and our country, and how we have turned our backs on all that he stood for on the one hand, but also because of my attachment to you, but if I feel I am not doing justice to our first prime minister I will seek your indulgence and withdraw.

'Let me finish by wishing you a very happy and rewarding new year. Inshallah I will be able to spend much more time with you picking your brains. Warmest regards, Kiran.'

I wrote back on 1 January 2015: 'Dear Kiran—Do please write about Nehru—your perceptions and emotions and whatever else you care to put in. Ravi Singh [Speaking Tiger's publisher] has asked me to write an introductory essay to the series. It is important for our voices to be raised in the present horrifying political climate. All the best to you and Tulsi.[4] Affly, Nayantara.'

So began, unexpectedly, a regular exchange by email or phone of our daily doings, family news, ideas and feelings, in a long-distance relationship where meetings were confined to literary occasions. I have gone back and forth through our mails to share some glimpses of a writer unlike any other and the closeness and comradeship that grew out of our keeping in touch. These mails also reveal how two writers reacted to the destruction of the secular democracy that India had hard-built and cherished since independence.

In 2015, I was invited to the Karachi Literature Festival. I wrote to Kiran on 3 January: 'I have to go to Karachi in early February and then will spend a couple of weeks in Chandigarh with my daughter-in-law, Franca, and two grandsons who will be visiting from abroad. Yesterday I was much preoccupied with thoughts of my son Ranjit who died on New Year's Day 2014. You mentioned my "iron will" and some of that helps in coping with his absence, and otherwise I try to cope by writing. And yes, one is terribly despondent about what goes on in our beloved country but this is the time to speak out, be heard, and not give up.'

Kiran replied the next day: 'I am singularly at a loss to understand how one copes with the death of someone so close, so dear, and so irreplaceable. While I do firmly believe in your iron will, I cannot underestimate the pain of your loss, and the worst of it is that while I would genuinely like to share your sorrow and pain, there's no way one can avoid the loneliness of the suffering. As to your Karachi trip, I hope intensely that it will come through. I have no idea how to hammer some sense into the two neighbours but I hope to God that this government is not going to escalate the already volatile tensions with its macho rhetoric.

'Would you be offended if I told you that I miss you? Warmest regards, Kiran.'

'No, I'm not offended,' I wrote back, 'it's nice to be missed.'

Then followed this exchange:

8 January 2015:

'Dear Nayantaraji—this is a spur of the moment email. A long time back, 1977 to be precise, I wrote a play called *Bedtime Story* during the Emergency. It is an abrasive play and proved to be very controversial and was banned both legally and extra-legally. Four times a prestigious publishing house said they would publish it but backed out. There is now some talk of publishing it though I will believe that when and if I see it in print in bookshops. Three questions: 1. Would you care to read it? 2. If you hated it, would you say so to me? 3. If you liked it would you write a quote? If you don't like to write quotes for books, I will certainly understand and not take it amiss.'

11 January:

'Kiran, I have just read your powerful play. Here is my quote: "Take a new look at the Mahabharata. *Bedtime Story* converts it into powerful theatre in a play that jolts us into thinking again about beliefs we consider sacred."'

12 January:

'How kind of you to read my play though you are so tight for time and overworked. I have only two shop-soiled and worn out words to show you how grateful I am: thank you.

'I have been reading *This Time of Morning*[5] in the insomniac hours of 2 a.m. to 5 a.m. I am an infernally slow reader and sleeplessness slows me down even further, but I marvel at your grasp of the bureaucracy, its men of integrity and those who hunger for power and the good life (not to mention the ambitions of their wives). Your portrayal of Kalyan Singh is a rare and invaluable contribution to our understanding of a man who is driven and truly dangerous for the polity.

'This is getting to be shamelessly repetitive but I do miss you very much. Warmest regards, Kiran.'

To my worry about his chronic insomnia he replied: 'I am an old hand at it ...My theme song in the meantime does not change. I miss you intensely. I miss you because I respect you very much. I love your name, your innate dignity, your passion for literature and politics and the strength of your convictions. If I were to speak of your beauty, I would be speaking as much about your mind as your person. I get tongue-tied when I am talking to you, but if you won't get offended, let me say you are very dear and precious to me, and I am very grateful that I came to know you. Oddly enough I am also very conscious of the fact that I am a zero conversationalist and have no social graces.

'P.S. Will try not to bother you for twenty-four hours at least.'

'"Social graces" and "conversation" should not matter very much between us,' I wrote, 'and we should try to meet and get to know each other better. Let me know about your coming Zurich visit. I have asked the Nehru Memorial Library to postpone the book event to 5 August.[6] That may make it easier for you to be there. But if you can't, or if you are feeling low or unwell, don't worry. I hope all goes well with your life in far-off Mumbai.'

In response, Kiran wrote: 'I am trying to figure out ways to reduce the distance between Mumbai and Dehradun to a twenty-minute bus ride.

'It is past eleven at night and I have just finished reading your introduction to *Nehru's India.* What a fine mind you have and how quietly but forcefully analytical. You have written a remarkable, informative and insightful essay. I wish it was much longer. It's a good thing I'm not in Dehradun just now for to your horror I would have hugged you and told you how much this thoughtful and succinct introduction meant to me.'

'Dear Kiran,' I wrote back, 'I have wondered how my introduction would go down with the essayists who have contributed to the volume. If they react as positively as you have, I will feel rewarded.

'Request: Please drop the "ji"—it's so formal. Affly, Nayantara.'

Kiran's response: 'Dear Nayantara—I have dropped the "ji" but I am not so sure about its removal. About going to Zurich, there is some chemical imbalance or some other problem leading to my chronic insomnia, and that is what the doctor, an extraordinarily kind man, wants to look into. Love, Kiran.'

2 July 2015:

'Dear Nayantara—I reached Zurich yesterday and have seen one of the doctors today. He is an amazingly kind human being and regarded as one of the best in Europe. I have no idea why he has agreed to see me when his would-be patients would pay a fortune to be treated by him. He said he would try to help but is doubtful if a few sessions would achieve any results. My apologies for not writing earlier but while lifting my suitcase I seem to have damaged my elbow and find it very painful to type. I am touched by your concern and good wishes and I look forward to being with you in August. I'll miss hearing your voice as much as I'll miss you. Love, Kiran.'

14 July:

'Dear Nayantara—I have just heard that HarperCollins will launch the third book of my Ravan & Eddie trilogy in Delhi on 4 August. *Rest in Peace* is a very peculiar rollercoaster ride and you won't miss anything if you are busy that evening. Besides we will be together at the Chandigarh festival.

'When did you get time to read *God's Little Soldier* when you are so busy yourself? Love, Kiran.'

I wrote back: 'What happy news. So glad I'll be there for the launch. Of course I have read GLS. Your writing is of absorbing interest to me. I have read two other of your novels, *Cuckold* and *Ravan & Eddie*, but not the second book in the trilogy—hadn't heard of it till you told me. How is your German trip going? Love, Nayantara.'

From Zurich Kiran wrote on 23 July: 'Dear Nayantara, I have been singularly remiss but I didn't wish to worry you. Today is the sixteenth day my fever has not gone down. Forgive me for not writing but I am a wreck and sitting up—barring the long visits to Le Charite, perhaps the most important hospital in Europe for tropical diseases—seems beyond me. I was in Stuttgart where I was examined and tested extensively, but there too they were unable to say what the problem was and how to tackle it. Till yesterday even the Charite people in Berlin would not venture any opinion except that favourite safe bet, a rare viral infection. This morning the elderly doctor called a friend who has been taking me to the hospital and said they are going to do some bacterial tests on my blood along with culture and she has started me on typhoid medication just to be on the safe side. Dear Nayantara, I miss you intensely. Love, Kiran.

'P.S. Finally news of a diagnosis. Believe it or not it's typhoid. They're starting intravenous treatment today.'

Later: 'I am finally on the mend since this morning but worn out to the point that I will do anything not to get out of bed. But there is one exception. I would walk miles to be with you, never mind in what state I reached.'

I wrote back: 'Dear Kiran—I had no inkling till now that you were so ill. To think that you have been going through this terrible time. It is a relief that it has been diagnosed at last. I gather, though you have not said so, that this is part of a long-standing illness. I suppose it is not the first time you have been through a virtual collapse of this kind. I am glad you have told me about it. I hope the treatment will restore you to normalcy and you will get back your strength. I feel dreadful about what is obviously a serious ongoing condition. I send you lots of love and lots of strength for your recovery—Nayantara.'

From Kiran on 31 July 2015: 'I had to spend the whole day in the hospital today before being given a discharge. God willing I leave tomorrow morning and will see you in Delhi on Tuesday.'

Back in Mumbai after the Nehru event[7] in Delhi he wrote: 'All my life I have thought of myself as damaged goods. I have spoken to you about my childhood and later years. It is in that context that I have always been grateful to God when the people I love and respect accept me despite my glaring faults. Life does strange things to us. One of them is our coming to know each other. What can I say beyond a big thank you. Love, Kiran.'

He went abroad for treatment again in April the following year. From there, he wrote: 'It's really sad that you are not here. It is very cold today and it would have been marvellous to have been with you watching the paintings in the sky. The air here has to be breathed to realize how wonderful it is and I think my lungs are certainly better. Unfortunately the problem with the lungs continues as well as my acute weakness and the absence of energy. The doctors say it's going to take time and that my impatience makes things worse and they still have not been able to tackle the problem of insomnia because that will take at least six months and they want to concentrate on the lungs first.

'May a day dawn soon when I will get up fresh and raring to go and land up in Dehradun. Lots of love and as usual missing you like crazy.'

'I am actually glad you are not in India,' I wrote. 'The heat and pollution are on the rise and we are told the summer is going to be the hottest in India and worldwide. Are you in hospital or staying elsewhere?'

'A very brief answer,' he replied. 'I have to be admitted to the hospital for tests off and on, but while staying in Berlin is expensive, Zurich is exorbitant. My school friends are convinced that I should find out why hyperactive Nagarkar now lies in bed the whole time.'

On 6 May 2016 came a lyrical letter from the hospital: 'The sun is out and as I lie in bed I am going for a walk with you. Is there a green more dazzling, bountiful and soothing than the spring largesse on a tree? Some years ago I had written about the utterly selfless generosity of trees, their shade, their fruit, the constant separation of carbon dioxide which leaves the air so much purer. The earth we walk on is stable because the roots of trees are the network that grip the soil and keep it from turning to landslides. I was born in Bombay and we had two jackfruit trees at our front door. They did not bear fruit for decades and then one day I came back from Pune to find low-hanging jackfruits on both trees. Talk about miracles. Even then trees played no role in my life. And then one day without notice they suddenly came alive and I started a torrid love affair with them. It is beyond me how we are willing to butcher them. I have little doubt that you must have been a beautiful tree in your past life.'

I replied: 'What a beautiful letter. Like everything you write it tells me so much about you. But this one is unique and it gladdens my heart. Thank you for taking me on this lovely walk. Thank you for your "and one day without notice..." And for making me a tree in my last life. The only sad part of your letter is "As I lie in bed". I long for you to be up and resuming normal activity and for us to share some time together. Much love, Nayantara.'

I came to know Kiran, who had suffered illness, pain, and bouts of long lonely hospitalization during his childhood, and lived with the reality of more to come, as a man with an undiminished zest for life, a writer of genius known for the vigour and vitality of his writing, and his novels for their ribald riotous humour, their hallmark eroticism, and their gut-wrenching portrayal of the subjugation of women. His own unprivileged background made the marginalized, the brutalized and the helpless the central focus of his fiction. I came to admire a man whose answer to his daunting health problems was to make light of them, enjoy and engage with life and live it to the hilt. The last line of his last novel, *The Arsonist*, proclaims: 'There is only one God. And her name is life.' If Kiran had a religion, it was this.

'Now why wasn't I in Dehradun last evening?' he wrote on 5 January 2016, 'Would have loved to have seen *The Great Dictator* with you. It's decades since I watched the Charlie Chaplin classic.'

I wrote: 'It would have been great to see it together and laugh together in this otherwise grim time. Love, N.'

There was no respite from recurring afflictions. Anxious, and now involved with his health, I asked him to keep me informed about it.

From Udaipur where he and Tulsi were attending a wedding (of, I believe, one of her family) in early

2016, he wrote: 'Udaipur is bearable in terms of the cold. As to the various functions of the wedding, everybody is very kind but I am the usual fish out of water. The wedding must have cost a bomb and a half but it was done with very good taste and understatement. The main problem was me since I went from bad to worse in terms of my lungs… Fortunately I was in touch with my doctors and was able to bring the problem under control.'

'My silence has nothing to do with my not writing to you,' he once wrote. 'The air in Mumbai is very bad and as usual I don't want to be left out of the competition in the matter of health problems. The pollution has done wonders for my operated eye, and I am amazed you haven't heard me cough all the way in Dehradun.' He said he might have to move for a while out of polluted Mumbai to some place where his breathing might be easier and I offered him and Tulsi my home in Dehradun, saying it was not the Ritz but a refuge if the need arose. 'No it's not the Ritz,' he replied, 'it's the ten-star home of someone far too precious to talk about. Any time I listen to music, read something special, or see a film like *The Third Man*, I am doing it with you. Missing you horribly.'

'Please don't apologize for intruding on my time,' he assured me, 'you never intrude on my time. I think you know very well how much you mean to me and how much I value you.'

This mail from him moved me profoundly: 'I don't have to wake up to have your name on my tongue or echoing in my head. In Marathi we say "devache nav ghya" and "diwas suru kara"—take God's name and start the day. There's also one other name I've discovered that helps to get a good start for the day. Love, sleepless Kiran.'

☙

We discovered our like-mindedness in our heartfelt support for Palestine and our abhorrence of the policies of Netanyahu[8], Donald Trump, and others of their ilk.

Of Israel's bombings and occupation of the West Bank, Kiran wrote in August 2017: 'Dear Nayantara and friends—when you mention Palestine and what Israel has done to those dear people, something snaps in me. My heart and acute commitment have always been with them. What I have learned over the years is that appalling suffering does not make us wiser or better folks. I could break my head on a rock over what Hitler did to the Jews, and yet the perennial question remains: Never again for whom? Just for the Jews or for every human being on the planet? And now we are faced with the same dilemma. What ghastly crimes will we commit in Kashmir, how soon will we see more appalling suffering and wars?'

We shared our grief at the assaults being made on freedom of expression and on our fellow citizens. We mourned the vanishing liberty, equality and democracy we cherished and were admired for around the world. We made our views public in interviews and articles. 'Just back from yoga,' I wrote, 'and have just read your letter to Jaitley[9] [*see p. 129*]. It says absolutely everything. A wonderful and satisfying read. I hope it has been widely read and that some cow-rakshak brought it to Jaitley's notice. I'll come and visit you in jail.'

He answered: 'The letter to dear Jaitley disappeared within a couple of hours but I was lucky that I could send it to you. I will not ask what I would have done if I had failed to befriend you. I will only thank God and you for your great warmth and generosity of heart. As always I learn so much from you every day. Your ethical compass is what makes you so rare and invaluable.

'This is a bit of a difficult time for me. I am trying to reduce my cortisone intake and that is always a delicate and tough downhill ride, and there is the business of us having to very likely move house. Love, Kiran.'

The changes that were taking place around us and the public indifference to mob lynchings and other barbarisms became our personal as well as political wounds. 'I have had to fight serious depression,' Kiran wrote, 'I no longer understand the species to which you and I belong. I don't know where we got the notion that mankind belongs to something called civilization.'

On 1 July 2017, I wrote to Kiran asking if he had read Harsh Mander's account in the *Indian Express* of the fifteen-year-old Muslim boy Junaid's ghastly murder by Hindutva fanatics on a train. In response, he wrote: 'Yes, I did read his article. I want us one and a quarter billion Indians to embrace the families of those who have been lynched or butchered, and those who murdered them or watched the murders in silence, brought to fast action courts, and that includes all those who watched or ordered the murder of a thousand Muslims in Gujarat, and hundreds of dear Sardarjis and Sardarnis in 1984, and those Muslims whom we murdered in the wake of the Babri Masjid demolition. Harsh Mander is one of the very few left in this country who take the duties of a citizen extremely seriously. May he wake up our comatose consciences and find millions of followers who will live up to the ideals of Gandhi, Martin Luther King, Jawaharlal Nehru and Mandela.'

I forwarded Kiran the letter I had written to Harsh Mander and the reply Harsh sent me: 'Dear Harsh—You are so right to mourn the apathy, indifference or connivance of the onlooker. Even those who care are often inhibited from speaking or helping out of fear in the present dangerous political climate…But one observation. What you are doing should be made public, or your yatra will remain a private act of solace and contrition and not make the impact it should. You are not embarked on a private matter of conscience. It is a revolt against all that is going on.'

Harsh replied: 'Thank you for your deeply valued words of solidarity and your wise counsel. I realize this is a very public revolt. We will work towards keeping it public. Please take care of yourself. You are precious. Best regards, Harsh.'

Kiran reacted: 'Love you and how for your amazing clarity and commitment to the cause of peace and the fight against vile actions and violence.'

I replied: 'The same can be said of you and of all your fiction.'

As a relief from what I had called the 'unmaking of modern India', we ridiculed the nonsense our rulers were making of history. I wrote to Kiran: 'I know you will be happy to hear that Maharana Pratap Singh won the battle of Haldighati against Akbar and that Akbar is no longer Great.'

Kiran replied: 'Yes, Akbar was a nobody, an upstart, a villain. Never forget Haldighati was the greatest battle ever fought and Akbar went down on his knees and begged for his paltry life. Lata Mangeshkar and all the RSS and BJP icons in my state now say with a raised flat right hand against the chest, *Jai Bharat, Jai Rajasthan*, and *Jai Maharashtra*. Please stand up and kindly do the same.

'The news (the good Lord help us) is that Prakash Clueless Javedkar is going to be the human resources minister. Oh where have all the good Maharashtrians disappeared? How come there is no Gokhale, or Agarkar, or Jyotiba Phule, or Ranade around?'

'Kiran,' I once wrote, 'I have just been watching on my laptop Emilio Pericoli singing my favourite song "Al di La", and then Sophia Loren dancing the Mambo Italiano. Felt like dancing myself. Hey Kiran, will you dance with me?'

Kiran: 'Will dance 24x7 with you. I'm flying to Dehradun right away.'

'Al di La' later found its way into a party scene in my novella *The Fate of Butterflies*.

Kiran: 'Just discovered Vividh Bharati which of late broadcasts non-stop horrendous ads on toilets, suddenly started a programme on K.L. Saigal, who I inherited from my mother, and who should I think of but you: "Main kya janu in naino mein kya jadu hai."'

From me: 'Saigal is a favourite of mine. You've reminded me of a song I love and some of the lines came back to me. What better way could I ask to be remembered!'

We spent time with each other's books and discussed them. Kiran thought I would not enjoy *Extras*—second in the Ravan & Eddie trilogy—and told me not to read it. 'I am now starting *Extras*,' I replied, 'Ravan and Eddie are an addiction—like booze—and I am hooked.'

Later: 'I am on page 292 of *Extras*. The tango with Mrs Fernandes was wonderful. So was Ravan and Eddie's dance with Helen. And I feel quite battered and bruised by the terrible things Three Point One does to poor Ravan. I am surprised that no reviewer has ever noticed your celebration of women in all possible ways, including the cheerful nymphomaniac whom you have wickedly named Sita.'

Still later: 'I finished *Extras* last night and found it as engrossing as the other two. At the end Belle's Cole Porter-Asmaan act is lovely. I am a Cole Porter fan myself and put a bit of a lyric of his in my novel *Lesser Breeds*. I specially love "You're the Top":

> You're the Nile, you're the Tower of Pisa,
> You're the smile on the Mona Lisa
> I'm a worthless cheque, a total wreck, a flop,
> But if baby I'm the bottom, you're the top.
> You're the top, you're Mahatma Gandhi,
> You're the top, you're Napoleon brandy
> You're the purple light of a summer night in
> Spain....

After reading *Rest in Peace,* the last in the Ravan & Eddy trilogy, I wrote: 'You had to kill Ravan and Eddie in the end but as characters they will live on and on. A great triumph.'

'Thank you so much, Nayantara, and thank you for following Ravan and Eddie. I was afraid that the surreal-plus-Bollywood-spoof-crammed ending would put you off. I have been so unsure of myself about *Rest in Peace,* your email gave me heart. On another note, this Thursday the Nehru Centre in Mumbai will have a discussion on the Nehru book[10] you edited. Since I know the director, Satish Sahani, an ardent but discerning Nehru disciple, I have been invited. The one person missing will be you. Love, Kiran.'

I replied: 'Dear Kiran—Regarding your writing my words are not kind. They are a matter of critical judgement. [A reference to my previous mails commenting on his work.] I am not sorry I won't be there for the Nehru book discussion. I have become too fraught about the Modi and Co. attack on Nehru and must try to distance myself intellectually and emotionally from it. Am snowed under with much to attend to, but love to you and my abiding love to Ravan and Eddie. Nayantara.'

'I see the sense of not allowing the whole orchestrated campaign of the current government to erase Nehru from our history and thus from memory not get to you, and I doff my cap to your sane and wise distancing from the current madness. Love, Kiran,' came the reply.

When *Jasoda* came out, he wrote saying, 'I've got the willies about this book. It's so different from my earlier work and in some ways very stark and unrelenting that just between you and me I am as usual unsure of myself. What was important to me was that Jasoda's husband gets what he wants, yet cannot hold on to his ill-begotten wealth and is shameless enough to return to Jasoda when he has squandered all his money and power. Perhaps it is the first time that Jasoda shows she is the agency which will obliquely not allow him to destroy her family.'

I wrote him my impressions: 'This is a stark and shocking story…The woman angle in *Jasoda* is frighteningly real with endless pregnancies and infanticides—frightening because this is accepted as a woman's lot along with every other kind of abuse. You have made a unique contribution to literature, but to mention just one aspect of it, this fierce and unsparing light you have thrown on the ugly condition of women. It baffles me that you feel unsure about *Jasoda*. You say you wrote this book intermittently and not continuously. I wonder if the ending might have been different if the narrative had been continuous? For me it was hard to believe that Aleksa who loved Himmat could have left him. I could instead see Himmat, now free of his tragic past and finally delivered from it. A more powerful ending perhaps?'

To this Kiran responded: 'Thank you so much for dissecting my novel and also stating clearly where you think I went wrong. As to Himmat, he is truly a man who has matured and is the only worthy male apart from Batlivala and Suyog, but I do believe he is unfortunately damaged goods.'

'The continuing shadow over your character Himmat,' I persisted, 'in spite of all that his mathematical genius has led him to achieve and the total transformation it has brought about in his life—is actually the continuing shadow over K. Nagarkar. But as you so well know, much can happen in fiction that cannot in life—which is why I wished Himmat had walked free of his author's past. You once told me you feel "low in self-esteem" and that you "wasted a lot of life". This lack of belief in yourself is absurd and has no basis in fact. I admire all that you and your writing stand for, as also the fortitude with which you face the terrible trials you are made to bear. I am proud of you. Be proud of yourself.'

I told him I was especially interested in reading his Marathi novel *Seven Sixes are Forty-three*, 'partly because there are hardly any—I can only think of Nabokov and Conrad—who have been successfully bilingual. Apart from that, it was your first novel, which may help me to understand the Kiran Nagarkar of that time. What you call its "fragmented structure" sounds interesting too. My only regret is that I cannot read it in Marathi though I am half Marathi, the other half Kashmiri.'

Kiran sent me the English translation and I wrote: 'I can now see the suffering child and the yearning young man you were. And your inborn awareness of people and conditions. *Seven Sixes* seemed to me a haunting tale of love, loss, and yearning, and of the "loner" you are—which is how you have described yourself to me.'

I had read *Cuckold* after I met him but re-read it, was struck afresh by its powerful storytelling, surprised once again by its perfect, artful ending, and couldn't believe that this novel, awarded in India and judged the literary masterpiece it was, had not been similarly recognized worldwide—which spoke ill of the neglect of its promotion outside of India.

Because we knew each other's work we were able to present it at litfests where we shared a session. Of one that we were to attend in Chandigarh, Kiran wrote: 'Mitulji wanted me to deal with one of your books but I have suggested we should highlight your enormously significant contribution to both Indian fiction and non-fiction.' At a litfest in Mumbai I described *Ravan & Eddie* as the fourth Indian epic, after the Ramayana, Mahabharata, and our epic Gandhi-led fight for freedom.

'Dear Nayantara,' wrote Kiran on 10 October 2015: 'Your strong actions have elicited reactions from the PM. Does he mean it? As my maternal uncles would say "ghoda maidan door nahin." Let's hope things will truly improve.' [*See p. 95.*]

'The PM has said nothing about the murders[11],' I replied, 'only repeated generalities. I am grateful for all the support I have had from friends and strangers and the wide coverage in the press and on TV, and I have ignored the crude and abusive attacks on the social media. I think I must have survived my eight-hour operation for cancer two years ago so that I could speak out against Hindutva's reign of terror. But I have never felt so terribly alone.'

In fact, companioned by our mails with their news of our daily lives, I was not alone. 'Sitaram Yechury rang,' I wrote, 'greeted me with Lal Salaam, came over, and said he had had a well-attended public meeting here in Dehradun. I was delighted to see him and we spent close to an hour chatting.' Another time: 'Vrinda Grover[12] is here to speak at the Mussoorie Academy. She came over and spent the evening and I got much interesting and distressing news from her over chilled white wine.'

From Kiran: 'Last night on NDTV I lost my temper. The anchor was treating me like a dumb prop and Makarand Paranjpe[13] was hogging all the time. The anchor himself was framing the debate in such a juvenile manner that I lost it and I have no excuse for my behaviour.'

I replied: 'I have just spoken to Githa Hariharan[14] who watched the programme and she said Paranjpe had hogged the time and you were quite right to react as you did. There are times when one must lose one's temper and this was one of them, so don't regret it. I've suggested to Githa that we (Indian Writers' Forum)[15] send out a statement in solidarity with Kanhaiya Kumar[16] and the thousands of students who heard and cheered him. I hope you saw it on TV.'

Earlier, in May 2015, I had written: 'Dear Kiran, I am getting a bit nervous about my session at a litfest at Hay-Wye[17]. It is called "The Crisis of the West", whatever that is supposed to mean. I will be up against the former speech writer for Tony Blair and a black British Tory who is a great empire lover. I hope I will be able to deal with the pair of them.

'How are you? I think of you, wonder how you spend your day, whom you meet, and so much else.'

From Kiran: 'Your qualifications for the encounter with Tony Blair's speech writer and the black empire-loving MP are very high and quite deadly. The Middle East and the world would not have been in such a colossal mess if Blair had not played lackey and been such a mendacious echo chamber for the supremely ignorant and war-mongering George Bush, Cheney, Rumsfeld.[18] Let's not forget the financial mess this wonderful team left behind. As if that was not appalling enough, Obama[19] backed all the conservative advisers, not to mention his secretary for finance and Larry Summers[20], and not one of all the massive fraudsters and bankers was punished for his crimes, on the totally bogus pretext that the biggest banks would collapse. We owe the refugee crisis and the climate crisis to Bush and the Republicans, but Obama too is partly responsible because he had the chance to take drastic steps when he first stepped into the presidency and let the Republicans get their way when the American public was so fed up with them. As to the empire lover, just remind him of the bloody mess in the Middle East including Netanyahu's Israel, fully backed by the

US, UK, Pakistan and others. You are a marvellous, thoughtful, and sharp speaker without ever losing your quiet dignity. So sock it to them, madam.'

'Thank you for your letter, Kiran, with its powerful indictment of the general state of affairs with which I agree in all respects. I don't have your high opinion of my "qualifications" but I feel strongly supported by your encouraging words. I think I will take the line that the crisis of the West is the paradox of the West itself, that its cherished values of liberty, democracy etc are for itself alone and do not apply to others, and to add to its sins, in an attempt to appear multicultural, the West makes deals with the worst elements in Islam and Hinduism.'

As it happened, unavoidable circumstances prevented me from taking part in this literary meeting.

ᴄᴈ

In June 2015, Kiran wrote to me about his friend and translator, Rekha, 'who is a Sanskrit scholar, one-time theatre and occasional film actress and theatre producer. She has been operated for cancer and has not been doing well at all, so a friend of hers and I have been doing day and night duty. Her knowledge of Hindu mythology, the Puranas, the epics, is phenomenal. I have been indebted to her as one of the most reliable reference sources in town… It's only now that I can understand what you have been through'—a reference to my surgery for cancer in 2013.

In July: 'My translator is going through a bad patch and I have been on duty between eight and ten hours a day and have to sometimes take her to the doctor…She is something of a messiah when it comes to animals. There was a time when she had three dogs, five or six turtles, plus cats. Now she has only one dog called Anarkali. For the first time in my life I now have an incredibly demonstrative lover. Anarkali goes berserk barking her head off when I ring the bell and despite all my placing my feet firmly on the floor and waiting for an assault, she has twice jumped on me and knocked me to the floor with her two paws on my face.'

'I can picture Anarkali's demonstrative love for you,' I replied. 'What can I say about the suffering your friend is going through. It is terribly sad and your devoted care of her is all that a friend's should be. You are so involved in the hopelessness and sadness of it that I'm very aware of it all.

'I generally cope with difficult times by writing, which is what I have been doing, and it feels good to be working on fiction after a long time and something seems to be emerging.'

From Kiran: 'I have been missing you terribly, horribly, miserably, but have been doing my male nurse duty every day.' I told him I was missing him too.

During Rekha's ordeal I received two books of poetry from Kiran—*Jejuri* and *Kala Ghoda Poems*—by his famous friend and close companion of twenty-five years, Arun Kolatkar, who had died many years ago. 'I can't thank you enough,' I wrote, 'for all the trouble you have taken to obtain these for me.'

From Kiran: 'I am sorry it took so long to bring

you and Arun together. He was not very loquacious when he was in unfamiliar company but he had a terrific sense of humour and would come up with replays, or if you prefer, act out, Laurel and Hardy, Charlie Chaplin and Buster Keaton scenes with utter deadpan humour. He was a voracious reader of anything and everything from Pliny to Kabir to Tukaram to Herodotus and Homer.

'I finally managed to open the attachment you sent and I regret to inform you that I am instantly flying over to Dehradun and moving in with you. You are well aware of my relationship with huge trees. If you had not made the blunder of sending me this picture of your garden (may many more follow) you and your garden would have remained safe, but now it's too late. May your lovely abode remain green with those marvellous shady bodhisattvas.'

During the stress and strain of looking after Rekha, Kiran wrote: 'I've been thinking of Zum'—my grandson Ayan Joshi who was my daughter Gita's younger son, suffering from deep depression—'and in that context I remember my growing up years—did I really grow up? As you know I was a stupendous, all-encompassing 24x7 problem for my parents. Perhaps problem is the wrong word, nightmare might be a closer description. That I partook of the nightmare is of no consequence now.

I was not past my teens when my mother died and by the time I was thirty my father was dead. He had seen my Herculean attempts to get a bit of oxygen into my lungs in December of the previous year and then had the fatal accident. How forgiving parents are and to what extent they make sacrifices for their children. I worry about Zum as if I were him. His illness is of course of a different kind but just as, if not more, serious. I do so hope he will break through and gain a normal life.

'I can't even count the number of days, weeks would be more precise, I haven't stepped out into the microscopic garden that borders the seashore behind the former American consulate opposite where we live. I will try to give you a call tomorrow. The test results are out and as expected not very good. But if possible I would like to postpone the operation, let's see. I'm going to talk to my Swiss doctor friend tomorrow. Much love.'

From me: 'I am so touched by your concern for Zum, and for being the person you are. I continue writing. What started as a short story has become longer. The characters don't need me any more. They are doing their own thing. Much love, N.'

Kiran: 'What more can one ask of one's characters than that they ignore you. Nayantara, there are four people looking after Rekha—Tulsi, Abodh Aras who is the head of Welfare of Stray Dogs, Rekha's cousin who has come down from Belgaum, and me. For me, Rekha has been an unbelievably rich source of mythology, Sanskrit and the Puranas. Any time I was lost, I could call her up and be enlightened. She also produced *Bedtime Story*.'

On 26 September came the news: 'Rekha died last night. This is the time to be with you and in fact I am very much at your home in Dehradun, trying to figure out what this loss means to me with your help.'

'However expected this news was,' I wrote, 'it must be unbearable for you, and at a time when you must be coping with much else. That Rekha is spared further suffering is the only consolation, though nothing comforts at such a time. It seems that everything happens at once—too much to bear. My prayers are with you.'

The year 2015 ended with Kiran's letter of 25 December night: 'Forgive me for not writing but my insomnia is much worse and it does take a toll. Add to that my niece from Sydney arrived today and the day has been a little chaotic.' And mine of 26 December: 'Yesterday I went to lunch at my sister's, and on New Year's Day I will spend the day trying not to think. It seems a practical way of dealing with the memory of my son Ranjit's death on that day a year ago.'

I needed Kiran in 2019: 'I am grief-stricken with the news from Gita that our beloved Zum has taken his own life,' I wrote on 7 April. 'We wept much on the phone at the thought of Zum's suffering which must have led to this terrible death.'

Kiran replied: 'I just got back from the hospital where I had gone for a long session with two doctors, to find this horrible news. I am appalled and saddened and can only imagine what utter grief and incomprehension Gita and you must be suffering. Whatever I say will be inadequate and incapable of bringing solace to Gita and you. I am utterly at a loss.'

Kiran's mails had kept me company through the unending strain and sorrow I had shared with Gita during Zum's cruelly unrelenting depression, and treatments that had no cure for this highly gifted and sensitive young man who ended his suffering by taking his own life at the age of twenty-two. Kiran had written: 'However useless it may be, I am with you this morning and full day and every day. Please do not hesitate to ask me to fly over to you any time you want me to be with you.'

'It is wonderful to know you would fly here if needed,' I responded, 'I would not expect that but it is a great comfort to know of your love and support.'

'I have tried to call you at least a dozen times, Nayantara, only to be told I am beyond the reach of Airtel. I will do my best to call you from a friend's home…But enough of this. How are you? Is it dreadfully hot there? Mumbai is hot and humid and I miss you.'

'Dear Kiran—I have been in deep mourning. Zum's funeral was on 2 May in London. Gita and Franca have told me how beautifully it went, with the ceremony in a most beautiful chapel which seated 150 and was packed with Zum's friends, and our family and friends. Gita, Ruchir[21] and Kabir all spoke most movingly and so did many of Zum's school friends. Some of his poems were read out and the music he loved was played. Afterwards all gathered at a cricket club nearby for food and drink and happy memories of Zum. We are trying to get reconciled to his loss.'

The political situation in the country and the world cast its perpetual shadow over our exchanges. Some of Kiran's comments on the state of affairs:

'It is my firm but totally unfounded belief that watching movies is the cure for all the problems of the world…the Philippino president murdering three million of his people which, he tells us, will cure them of the drug habit; our macho grandstanding with surgical strikes without any concept of consequences. Has the world ever seen so many loonies operating at the same time? But where do I get to see five or six movies a day to sedate my nerves?

'I am carrying on not heroically but in a mundane and half-awake fashion. If there is any buoyancy, it is due to you. Most of all I am missing you, missing you, missing you. There is no dearth of things to love in you but one of the most important is your sense of justice and your fight for it. Hope we can meet soon, better still sooner than soon.'

'Thank you for sending me the Chomsky letter signed by 132 others. Let's see if it has any effect on our revered PM.'

'I know I am not supposed to say this even to myself but I have the feeling that our country and all of us who believe in the values enshrined in the Constitution are in for a frightening, vicious and very prolonged dictatorship…Here is what my Swiss doctor friend thought of your Hindu article: "This is really a fantastic text and a pleasure to read."' [A reference to my article, 'A Hindu Speaks', which appeared in *The Tribune* on 8 October 2017, *See p. 98.*]

Some of my comments:

'Yes, we are in an evil situation. What can we do except keep speaking up. Fascism is having a re-run in Europe too. And there is the Trump plus North Korea madness. Let's keep sane and strong, Kiran.'

'I have been saddened by the sudden death of Asma Jehangir, a brave and wonderful journalist and activist whom I last met at the Karachi litfest and she said, "Next time you must come to my home in Lahore."'

'I was appalled by the murder of Sujaat Bukhari in Srinagar—another courageous journalist killed. In view of the worsening situation there I have written to Sanjay Nahar (whose organization is giving me the Lal Dedh Award[22]), asking him to consider changing the venue of the award ceremony to Delhi.'

Demonetization, which wrecked the economy, dealt Kiran a vicious blow as it did to many others. 'Five days ago,' he wrote in November 2016, 'the money got over and I had no option but to stand in the queue at the bank. After being there for over four hours in the sun, without realizing it I hit the ground. Cross my heart I am much better now though of course the pollution poses other problems. I think of the farmers and all the other daily wage earners and my heart goes out to them, and my anger at the sheer thoughtlessness and utterly unnecessary haste of this measure drives me up the wall. Now please give me some happy and fun news. How are you?' I rang him immediately, horrified.

Around us Indian history was being erased, rewritten, fabricated. Writers had been assassinated. Cattle traders, a blacksmith, a dairy farmer, had been lynched by cow-rakshaks. Disagreement with the government was branded anti-Indian and charged with sedition. Mob violence ruled the streets. 'How many times can one's heart break?' I wrote to Kiran. 'Even drowning oneself in work doesn't help. But this book which I'm calling *The Fate of Butterflies* is half done. It's been "a hard day's night" as the Beatles put it, which is to say I am working hard and living in a world of my own. I have never written with such hellbent concentration. It's the times we live in and never knowing what tomorrow will bring. I am writing *Butterflies* to interest, amuse and divert you in all your troubles.'

'Let me say something that makes me dance off my feet into the blue sky,' wrote Kiran, 'I have no words to tell you how grateful I am for your love and affection. The thought that you are writing *The Fate of Butterflies* for me, to get me off my third-rate health problems, gave me a high that gets higher by the minute.'

This was followed by: 'Please forgive my silence since I have been running a temperature with a rotten headache and have been stalled in reading the pdf of *Butterflies*. I will get back to you as soon as I am better and have finished reading it.'

And next: 'Just finished reading it. It's brilliant, superbly told, and your encyclopaedic knowledge is astounding. The happy ending came as a surprise but there were parts in it that were searing. I don't ever want you to stop writing these incredibly relevant and enchanting stories which hold a mirror to the appalling nature of what is happening in our country. God knows how you pulled this and *When*

The Moon Shines By Day out of your magic box, that remarkable invisible thing called your superb mind.'

'Your comments are all that I could wish for,' I wrote. 'They make my journey through this novella—in these terrible times and under so much pressure—worthwhile. The ending is happy but also grim. The lovers have got together but caught up in the horror and tragedy of the times, which they can do nothing to change, they see the wisdom of Prahlad's poignant advice : "And so—let's dance!"'

I had dedicated *When The Moon Shines By Day* 'To Kiran—a great storyteller—this story of our times', and in place of a dedication for *Butterflies* I found a song from a 1936 Hollywood movie that expressed the spirit of the novella and sent it to Kiran:

> There may be trouble ahead,
> But while there's moonlight and music and love
> and romance,
> Let's face the music and dance!
> Before the fiddlers have fled,
> Before they ask us to pay the bill,
> And while we still have that chance,
> Let's face the music and dance!

Kiran: 'I love the song, so yes, please put it instead of a dedication, and let's face the music and dance!'

The year 2018 was a time of uprooting for Kiran and Tulsi. Leaving the gracious, spacious family-owned house in Mumbai which Tulsi's family had decided to sell, was painful for her. For Kiran it had been home since they became partners. They had invited me to dinner there when I was at a litfest in Mumbai not long after I met Kiran.

While still at the family home, Kiran wrote in January, 'Hope you got up to a lovely morning, Nayantara, unlike the smog-ridden opaque one in Mumbai. Since the guests in the house—members of Tulsi's family—are so ill, most of the time I am running around with Tulsi trying to get doctors and other help to look after them. Everybody but everybody is down with either pneumonia or acute lung problems and coughing like a chorus from purgatory.'

He wrote on 14 February: 'I got back last evening from Delhi—and will send you my speech to the

Sahitya Akademi awardees—to find that things have speeded up to the point where I find myself in a zombie mode. It appears that the buyer wants us to move out on the fifteenth of March and we do not know if we will have a place to stay in the long run. As to a temporary apartment that we will have to rent, so far we have absolutely no clue as to where to find one. Rents are so exorbitant that I have no idea how we are going to finance the whole change of life and lifestyle. As if all this was not enough to make me lie down and not want to get up, my brother Jyotee is in town and visited us for lunch—(incidentally we have no cook)—but it gets worse. The whole family of my cousin Shubha who translated *Seven Sixes* is visiting Mumbai. All six of them need, quite rightly, urgent and constant attention.'

'I've read your speech at the Sahitya Akademi with great interest,' I replied. 'Bits of it—your college days—were great fun to read—the gorgeous girls and others who came in chauffeur-driven cars etc. You skim casually over your own zero academic performance caused by serious illness and absence.

'I hope you are managing your family's visit without too much strain. I would have liked very much to meet your brother. It would fill in one of the gaps in my knowledge of your family and your past.'

'We are trying to settle in,' Kiran wrote on 1 April from the temporary residence they had found in Worli, 'but there's always something or the other we have not taken care of.'

I wrote the next day: 'Today is your birthday and I am thinking of you, wondering if you were born at home or in a hospital, wondering what you are doing to celebrate it, wondering about all that I don't know about you. Above all I am wishing you a happier year than the last one has been, in spite of all the uprooting and upheaval.' And on 12 April: 'This is just to say your article on Palestine in today's *Indian Express* is superb and much needed.'

From Kiran the same day: 'Just got back from a very lengthy meeting with a new doctor after having to wait three hours in the waiting room, and then going to hear the former Pakistani ambassador to the US whose new book *Reimagining Pakistan* was released today in Mumbai. He was truly remarkable and I missed you dreadfully.'

From me: 'How terrible that you had to wait three hours to see the doctor. I hope all is well and no new problems have arisen. What a time you are going through. I wish I had been with you to hear the Pak former ambassador. It is such a waste not being able to share these occasions which are of such interest to both of us.'

On 27 May: 'Dear Nayantara—I have very lame excuses to justify my silence. I have tried to call you at least a dozen times only to be told yet again that I am beyond the reach of Airtel. I will do my best to call you from the home of one of my friends. The other problem is my energy levels. I am having to do several blood tests but they do not suggest why I want to lie down all the time and feel so infernally weak. Apparently these are very elaborate tests which last for anywhere between one and a half to two hours and sometimes one is called again. It takes a few more days afterward before they hand over the diagnosis. I will keep you informed when I have some clear news. As to finding a permanent apartment, that is turning out to be a serious pain in the posterior. But let me say one simple thing. God has been very kind to me to allow me to know you and to bring me so close to you. Love, Kiran.'

On 9 June: 'The delay in getting back to you is due to two reasons. The damned tests had to be repeated and Dr Sorabjee said exactly what I have been fearing...that I will have to do many tests on various other counts...The second reason is that we have got new help called Santosh in the house. He had gone out when a mobike disregarded a red traffic light and flung our man on the back of his head. He has been badly injured and I spent till two a.m. last night at the police chowki. Throughout the day today I have been pestered non-stop by the relatives and friends of the man who hit our help. They want to hand over money for the recovery of Santosh on the condition that the case is withdrawn. I have told them over and over again what the police officer relayed to me, that once the case is registered with the police, it cannot be withdrawn.'

Later in June Kiran wrote: 'First of all, how are you? Not just your health but all the problems you and Gita are facing about the claims on your house[23]. Are your relatives and the land mafia still harassing you? The news from my side is merely to try and avoid getting worked up about looking for a permanent home plus the usual sing-song of fluctuations in my health plus the appalling humidity. The only lucky thing was that my brother and I talked yesterday and we both made sure not to enter any dubious or provocative subject.'

In July it was my turn to be ill and I wrote to Kiran: 'Thank you for ringing. I was feeling very depressed. Hope for the test results on Monday. It is a comfort to know that Noni[24] is coming on Tuesday.'

'Thank God Noni will be with you, but please don't hesitate to ask me to fly down. I will be waiting for Monday afternoon to hear what the doctor says. May everything turn out well, your tests and the house matter. Love.'

On 9 September: 'Dear Nayantara, I suspect both of us have been sent on a banwas (vanwas in Marathi). I hate it but it raises both my anger and yearning.'

Later that month: 'You had told me about your father translating three Sanskrit classics. However, reading your speech about the absolutely remarkable Lal Dedh, your Kashmiri connection and your father translating the Kashmiri classic *Rajtarangini* suddenly made a huge impact and came home to me. I am so happy and proud you were given the Lal Dedh Award.

'The Ganapati festival is on and the noise levels are beyond belief, but we Indians love noise and the louder the better. Added to the Hindu festivals, we have several masjids close by and each azan is not only louder than the neighbouring one and incredibly besura, that all my sympathies are with Allah for having to bear with such ghastly devotion. God willing we'll see each other soon.'

In October 2018 when the #MeToo movement was getting stronger, three women journalists alleged on Twitter—one of them anonymously—that Kiran had behaved inappropriately with them on separate occasions.[25]

Soon after, Penguin Random House cancelled its contract for his novel *The Arsonist.* Kiran issued a statement on 11 October utterly rejecting these accusations: 'Forgive me for not responding earlier to the women journalists who have accused me of sexual impropriety on Twitter. The news came as a complete shock to me. It took me time to try and digest the tweets. I unequivocally deny these allegations of sexual impropriety which go against the heart of my character and everything I stand for. I have never engaged in any such behaviour with anyone. I must stress that I do not wield any power or authority that would allow me to harm or hamper a professional journalistic career. Let me end by saying that long before the #MeToo movement came to the fore, I have always strongly supported women who have been subject to any kind of mistreatment. All my novels and plays are witness to my intense concern for the plight of women in today's times.'

Kiran had once told me his parents had wanted daughters but had two sons, so they had given their sons the names they would have given daughters, and treated a much-loved niece as their own. He and his brother had early seen that in their family men did not rule the roost.

He was deeply shocked by these ugly attacks on his personal integrity which also cast a shadow on his reputation as a writer. His struggle to cope with their effect on his health and his peace of mind became the tragedy of the last year and more of his life.

In November 2018, Kiran wrote: 'I am trying to fight my awful sleepless nights which now have to cope with my occasional rage about the #MeToo madness which is destroying so many careers and reputations. I am just grateful that I have you and some other very dear friends who have stood by me without ever thinking me capable of what the tweets accuse me of.'

I had taken a strong public stand against the

direction #MeToo had taken, the witch-hunt and sex-war it had become, and the fact that it had not raised its voice on behalf of the countless voiceless rural and urban women who live in domestic slavery and are sexually abused in the workplace which is their home. I made my views clear in a statement published in *Scroll.in* and in this short statement for interviews and public use: 'In a democracy no citizen is guilty because someone says so. The ripple effect of these say-so accusations is having the same effect as propaganda, which operates on the principle that if you repeat something often enough, it becomes true. This is not only unacceptable, it is making a mockery of the #MeToo movement.' I took this stand at a Bengaluru litfest in a session with my good friends, Shashi Deshpande (fellow panelist) and Shobhaa De (moderator), in opposition to them. #MeToo had demanded that litfests boycott any writer who had been named. I refused invitations to participate in any litfest that obeyed this diktat.

Kiran to me: 'I think of you as my armour against the world.'

Accusations—some mendacious—that the public accepted without question, and without a hearing from the accused, confirmed my opinion of the opportunity #MeToo had lost, to bring to light the stories of the beaten, bullied and battered women who live unprotected from routine domestic violence and sexual harassment and are powerless to seek help. The men responsible do not figure in any indictment, and the highly placed among them flourish, like the Supreme Court judge who himself headed an examination of the charges against him and absolved himself of any wrongdoing. Meanwhile the affected woman on his staff had been dismissed and grossly humiliated by being made to kneel, 'matha teko' before his wife, and apologize for daring to accuse him. Her family members had been hounded and their careers ruined. That some amends were made long afterwards made no difference to the savagery they suffered. Here was a lone woman who had fought alone and at great risk for her rights, for whom #MeToo should have raised an outcry but took no notice of.

My own response to the tweets was to ask Kiran to represent me in Pune to accept the first Bhai Vaidya Award[26] which had been set up in memory of the distinguished socialist politician's lifelong commitment to policies that served human, not market needs. Kiran was asked to speak on the occasion, in addition to my videoed speech.

2018 was also the year when, much to my joy, I connected with the Marathi literary scene. A Marathi publisher accepted my two novellas, *Moon* and *Butterflies* and an avant garde Marathi women's magazine published my short story 'Martand'.

'This is quite some story,' Kiran wrote to me about 'Martand'. 'It is short and yet says so much. And oddly enough its best quality is that one finds that all three characters—husband, wife, and lover—are good people and one sympathises with all three of them, including the husband. How I love your writing.'

The happiest news I received was that my father Ranjit Sitaram Pandit's translation—from Sanskrit into English—of the twelfth century Kashmiri classic *Rajtarangini*, had now been translated into Marathi. The prestigious Marathi Sahitya Sammelan—whose festivals celebrated Marathi writing from all over the country—invited me to address it. I welcomed this recognition of my father's Sanskrit scholarship and acknowledged the honour done to his memory in the emotional speech I wrote for the occasion, introducing my father as the freedom fighter he had been under Mahatma Gandhi's leadership, and dying in 1944 of his fourth imprisonment during British rule. I was to deliver it at Yavatmal on 11 January 2019, and sent it with its Marathi translation to Kiran for his reaction.

'Dear Nayantara—Nobody in India writes speeches as powerfully and with such intensity of feeling as you do. You do both your father and Marathi proud. We Maharashtrians were at the forefront of breaking all taboos and reinventing ourselves, just as the Bengalis did in the late nineteenth century. Gokhale, Agarkar, Ranade, Tilak, Karve, are but a few that come to my mind. But then came along the RSS and the Hindu Mahasabha—Savarkar and Golwalkar and Godse[27] and later on the shameless thug-party called the Shiv Sena. I hope to God the literary crowd at Yavatmal grasps the width and depth of your speech. It is truly one to remember. Love, Kiran.'

The speech was never delivered as I was disinvited by the state government. No official reason was given, but I was told that the then BJP-led Maharasthra government had put pressure on the organisers to cancel the invitation. But the Marathi translation by Prashant Talnikar was widely circulated and the *Indian Express* and *Scroll.in* also carried the full text of my speech [*See p. 104*]. I was overwhelmed by the resounding support I received from Marathi writers. Many boycotted the sammelan, others attended and condemned the state's action. The annual sammelans were organized by the Akhil Bharatiya Marathi Sahitya Mahamandal. Its chairman, Dr Shripad Balchandra Joshi—an eminent writer himself—rang me in tears to say he had resigned in protest. And I, too, was moved to tears by his visit to my home in Dehradun with his wife to express their solidarity with me. At a time when dissent was dangerous, Marathi writers had upheld the freedom of expression publicly, vociferously, and en masse. My admiration for them knew no bounds.

As liberty, equality and democracy took a hammering and we watched the destruction of all that India had stood for, it took determination to keep one's spirits up. 'I have been watching *Versailles* (a film on the reign of Louis XIV) on Netflix,' I wrote to Kiran. 'More hectic fucking than acting but it certainly takes one's mind off the state of affairs in India.' I also sent Kiran a picture that my cousin Jai Bhandarkar had sent me from the Pandit family archives in Mumbai.

'Zero sleep,' wrote Kiran, 'but imagine getting up to see you in that picture with your mother. You look so beautiful I cannot stop looking at it. God bless you for never letting this truly supernatural beauty come in the way of your pursuit of the Bhagvad Gita's ideal of doing the right thing regardless of success or failure.'

He made me laugh with: 'Love you, love you, love you, love you, love you, love you, love you, love you, love you, love you, love you, love you, love you, love you, love you, even as I lie low, and bathe, dance, stand on my head, think of you, look into the ever-stretching sea, grieve for our Mother Earth, lose hope, and hate myself for letting yours truly down and all this I do listening to K.L. Saigal and Pankaj Mullick.'

'This is like no letter ever written!' I replied. 'Shall I frame it and hang it up to look at every day? And you are like no other. Stay that way! Much love.'

I thought of Nehru's words: 'A government does not break its word' when in August 2019, the army occupied Kashmir, shut down communication and imprisoned political leaders along with all who protested against the government's lawless occupation, and its abrogation of Article 370 which accorded special status to the state of Jammu and Kashmir.

'I hold my head down in shame and anguish,' wrote Kiran. 'If we can treat our own brothers and sisters so shamefully, what can foreigners, neighbours and outsiders expect from us? Dear God, save our Kashmiri brothers, sisters and friends from this appalling dictatorship.'

'Truly a nightmare,' I replied, 'and there's more to come as they complete their destruction of the glittering aspiration that India once was. As you know, I share your heartbreak but I try not to despair. Regardless of the lies told here, it is some consolation that we are getting the facts of what is happening in Kashmir from the BBC and some leading newspapers abroad. And come what may we have to go on resisting the evil that we see. That doesn't mean we can't have a good cry when we meet.'

The *Times of India* asked me for my reaction to the abrogation of Article 370 in Kashmir. I sent my reply to Kiran: 'This action resembles that of a military dictatorship, not a democracy. It has been taken by a government that cannot tolerate a Muslim-majority state. Now it can proceed to Hinduize Kashmir, following the example of Israel which has flooded Palestinian territory, the West Bank, with Jewish settlers.'

We had talked about the difficulties of getting Kiran's novel *The Arsonist* published after Penguin Random House cancelled the contract, but the publishing house Juggernaut, ignoring #MeToo, stepped in and published it in June 2019, and it arrived as a surprise from Kiran.

I wrote: 'I have just finished your book with its fiery ending and its last gripping line: "There is only one God and her name is life." How great must have been your need to write this particular book at this particular time when all that is good and true is being bludgeoned to death, and the personal difficulties and pressures under which you managed to write it. Then your long connection with Kabir, manifest in *God's Little Soldier*, and long before that, as your very powerful Afterword makes clear, with Arun Kolatkar in your 25-year close companionship with him. And as you say, Kabir had got under your skin even before that. You owed Kabir this book and repaid your debt to him.'

Kiran was convinced reviewers would miss the significance of this book—which they did—and wrote to me: 'I saw your email last night and as usual I was taken aback by how incredibly perceptive you are...I would like to deny the dreadful damage those tweets have done me but I am so grateful that you can see through me. I am conscious that somewhere along the line I am a broken person but I am truly beholden to you for giving me the courage to try and put myself together again.'

He wrote an article—'Dishonouring an International Agreement'—about the dangers threatening West Asia and the possibility of war as a result of Trump's America dishonouring the international nuclear deal that America along with other countries had made with Iran—a subject not being adequately reported in our press. He sent it to two publications. Neither replied. #MeToo, he wondered? He agreed to one more try and the *Indian Express* accepted it, but it was put aside when the Kashmir news blotted out much else. The dangers Kiran had spelled out continued to rise.

He and Tulsi had finally moved into a permanent home, an apartment in the familiar surroundings of her old family home, and Tulsi later told me she had placed Kiran's desk in front of a window facing the sea as he liked looking out on it. Of my forthcoming November visit to the Tata litfest in Mumbai, Kiran wrote: 'It will be marvellous to meet.'

He died on 5 September 2019.

A permanent tribute to Kiran, who especially valued invitations from universities and contacts with young readers, came from Mitul Dikshit, founder of the Chandigarh Literary Festival and the Dikshant Global School, when the school named its newly built library after Kiran. The school, along with us invited guests, celebrated the opening of the library with a rousing programme of music and song. In 2019 the Chandigarh litfest held a memorial opening session in his honour where Tulsi and I both spoke.

I recalled what Kiran had written not long after our first meeting: 'You asked me how I could miss someone I had really met only once. That is a logical rational question. All I can say is some areas of our life and mind may not fit into this framework…I suspect despite all my cynicism I am an old-fashioned believer in either astral connections or bonds that are beyond the ken of human beings.'

Whatever the explanation for this unexpected and enriching encounter, it bears witness to two Indian writers facing the evil of their times—a time of ferocious attacks on India's people, traditions and institutions through public killings, the imprisonment of citizens inconvenient to the ruling power, and the throttling of dissent; all this made possible by a political class and its supporting elite who have no use for our civilizational heritage, and none for human rights or human life. If horror needs description or defining, here it is. We have seen, heard and read about it as it occurred and recurred.

In such a time nothing is more heartening than the knowledge that one is not alone in one's rage and defiance. As writers, we had this assurance from each other, and drew strength from the unending courageous protests by Indians who refused to be silenced. In the stand we ourselves took through the spoken and written word we joined forces with the fight against the unmaking of India.

Epilogue

This article, written by Kiran in 2005, and sent to me by Tulsi after his death, reveals his highly unusual, little-known and fascinating family background, leading him to reflect on how the rebel streak in his inheritance has influenced his life, his beliefs, and his literature.—Nayantara Sahgal

Looking for Gulbadan's Kite

Kiran Nagarkar

I never met any of my grandparents. So I ask myself, how did my paternal grandfather Balwant Nagarkar, a man who died a good thirty years before I was born, influence my life so considerably, and turn my face in the direction of the conscious and unconscious choices I would have to make for the protagonists and characters of my novels?

Yet what I know about him is precious little. He came from an orthodox Chitpavan Brahmin family from Ahmednagar. The word is that he was attached to a temple as a child to train to become a priest. He was a 'madhukari' , a boy who ate at certain fixed houses, a different one for every day of the week. The next thing you know about him is that he has joined Wilson College in Bombay. How? Did he have a rich patron? Did he come under the influence of some British missionary? Your guess is as good as mine. There is also some talk that he may have been asked to leave Wilson College for some paper he wrote on Christ.

The year is 1893. My grandfather goes to Chicago for the Conference of World Religions along with Swami Vivekanand. Vivekanand represents the Hindu faith, my grandfather but a minor branch of it: the Brahmo Samaj, which harked back to the monotheism of the Upanishads. From all accounts it appears that Vivekanand was the star of the day. My grandfather didn't make it that big, but he was invited once again to another Conference of World Religions in 1903.

Questions: What made him change his faith? What motivated him? Why would he give up the certainty and security of the Hindu faith, and the livelihood from a highly respected Brahmin priesthood? Why did he risk the appalling prospect of being kicked out of his community and be persistently shunned? Why did he choose to risk ostracism by crossing the shores of India not once but twice? But he hadn't had his fill of rebellion. After his first (or maybe it was his second) wife died, he married again, this time outside his community. He married a Jew. He had nine children with her. My father was the eldest and it was natural that he should give up his education before his matriculation and take up a job. He joined the Railways as a clerk.

I was four years old when, without realizing it, I felt the consequences of my grandfather's actions and choices. One of my father's childhood acquaintances had moved into Hindu Colony in Bombay where we lived. She had four daughters, the youngest one of whom, Mita, was my age. My parents would invite Mita to come to our flat to play with me. Every time she left, the parents of my closest friend who happened to live opposite would tease me about being Krishna and ask me how my 'gopis' were doing. It was thanks to them that I thought I was doing something that was not the done thing.

Somewhere it began to register in my mind that our family was different. We were Hindu but different from other Hindus. They worshipped the images of many gods. We had no images and we believed in only one God. What did I make of this? I'm not quite sure. All I can say with any certainty is that I began to dread going to temples, and to feel uncomfortable with the whole pantheon of three- or four-headed gods and goddesses with eight and sixteen arms. Instead of temples we went to the Prathana Samaj, the Maharashtrian version of the Brahmo Samaj to listen to a sermon interspersed with 'abhangs' and 'dohas'. It would only occur to me later on that the Brahmos were as much influenced by the Protestant forms of worship that had come with British missionaries as by the Upanishads.

After four years at a Marathi school I was sent to an English medium school run by priests. I spent six years at Don Bosco, yet during all that time I did not learn the school prayer that we were supposed to recite every day. For some reason I can't explain I mumbled some gibberish without intending any disrespect, and got away with it.

After school and then college, I found that I had begun to distance myself from both the monotheism of the Brahmos and the gods and goddesses of my Maharashtrian friends. I was well on the way to closing the doors on all religion and had begun to dislike organized religion with a passion.

And yet my novels and plays are the site of an almost obsessive concern with religion as they are of every kind of inter-, infra-, and counter-cultural conflict. Shri Krishna is at the heart of my play *Bedtime Story*. He appears in *Ravan and Eddie*, and is the kabab-mein-haddi between Meerabai and the Maharajkumar in *Cuckold*. *Seven Sixes are Forty-three* does not stray much outside the Hindu fold but it explores the cross-currents and conflicts within Hinduism itself. *Ravan & Eddie* is the story of two religions, two cultures running parallel but almost never meeting, seen through the eyes of two children, one a Hindu, the other a Catholic. *God's Little Soldier* is a journey through both Islamic and Christian extremism.

Sometimes I think my grandfather has put a curse upon me. I cannot believe yet I cannot leave well enough alone. I keep trying to exorcise him and yet I'm not sure if along with him my muse too will vanish. Who asked him to be a maverick and break out of the happy certitudes of the Brahmin priestly class? Why could he not have continued to toll the bells of his temple in Ahmednagar clangorously so I would hear, not have to confront the terrible dilemmas of our self-righteous violence, of Ram and Rahim, the touchables and untouchables, of Osama bin Laden and of Bush, of the terror of 9/11 and the tragic trajectory of the conflict between India and Pakistan, India and Palestine?

Where will I find Gulbadan's kite?

Twenty-five years ago, maybe it was thirty, I came across a biography of the Emperor Babur's daughter, Gulbadan. I learnt that she used to fly a kite with her brother Humayun. It was such an insignificant detail, but I sat there with a sense of utter wonderment and joy.

I felt that I was holding the string of the kite that Gulbadan flew and it stretched all the way to the Prophet Mohammed who surely flew kites and to Christ and to Prince Siddhartha who would become the Buddha. Gods come and go, for they too are subject to change. Great upheavals knocked out the matriarchal hierarchies of the Greek pantheon and replaced them with a patriarchal order. The Earth-mothers in India made way for Varun, and then Varun was replaced by Indra. Yet who really remembers and worships this one-time top honcho today? Easy come, easy go.

The only constant we can hold on to for dear life is Gulbadan's kite. It is our only hope. It's as if the future of mankind and this poor benighted planet of ours depends on it. So long as we are aware that all the four or five billion of the earth's denizens are flying that same kite, what matters what religion we practice, or to what caste or country we belong?

PART TWO

Bonds of Dissent

Two Writers in Protest

Nayantara Sahgal's letter dated 6 October 2015 to the Secretary, Sahitya Akademi, returning the award given to her in 1986 by the Akademi for her novel, Rich Like Us. *The letter was titled 'The Unmaking of India':*

6 October 2015

To: The Secretary
Sahitya Akademi
New Delhi

Dear Mr Sreenivasa Rao,

In a recent lecture, India's Vice-President, Dr Hamid Ansari, found it necessary to remind us that India's Constitution promises all Indians 'liberty of thought, expression, belief, faith and worship'. The right to dissent is an integral part of this Constitutional guarantee. He found it necessary to do so because India's culture of diversity and debate is now under vicious assault. Rationalists who question superstition, anyone who questions any aspect of the ugly and dangerous distortion of Hinduism known as Hindutva—whether in the intellectual or artistic sphere, or whether in terms of food habits and lifestyle—are being marginalized, persecuted, or murdered. A distinguished Kannada writer and Sahitya Akademi Award winner, M.M. Kalburgi, and two Maharashtrians, Narendra Dabholkar and Govind Pansare, both anti-superstition activists, have all been killed by gun-toting motor-cyclists. Other dissenters have been warned they are next in line. Most recently, a village blacksmith, Mohammed Akhlaq, was dragged out of his home in Bisara village outside Delhi, and brutally lynched, on the supposed suspicion that beef was cooked in his home.

In all these cases, justice drags its feet. The prime minister remains silent about this reign of terror. We must assume he dare not alienate evil-doers who support his ideology. It is a matter of sorrow that the Sahitya Akademi remains silent. The Akademis were set up as guardians of the creative imagination, and promoters of its finest products in art and literature, music and theatre. In protest against Kalburgi's murder, a Hindi writer, Uday Prakash, has returned his Sahitya Akademi award. Six Kannada writers have returned their awards to the Kannada Sahitya Parishat.

In memory of the Indians who have been murdered, in support of all Indians who uphold the right to dissent, and of all dissenters who now live in fear and uncertainty, I am returning my Sahitya Akademi award.

Yours sincerely,
Nayantara Sahgal,
Dehradun

A Hindu Speaks

Nayantara Sahgal

The other day an acquaintance of mine asked me why I was opposing Hindutva. What did I have against it? I told her why. I said I opposed it for two reasons. One reason is personal and the other is political.

Let me begin with the personal. I cannot accept Hindutva because I am a Hindu. By this I don't mean only that I was born a Hindu, but that I am a believer. My religion is important to me. I draw daily strength and sustenance from it. It is central to my life and thought, and to my behaviour toward believers of other faiths for sanatan dharma teaches that the world is our family. To millions of Indians, of whatever faith, religion matters. And all truly religious people know that God has no chosen people. We are all equal in the eyes of the Creator.

So it is unbearable to watch my religion being transformed into what it was never meant to be by people who call themselves Hindus but practise a brutal, militant creed of their own that drives them to lynch defenceless innocent Indians, pump bullets into those who question their creed, and enter a train armed with knives to stab to death a fifteen-year-old boy who is returning to his village after his Eid shopping in Delhi. Unbelievably, this vengeance pursues some of its victims beyond the grave. What else are we to make of the news that the grieving families of Mohammed Akhlaq and Pehlu Khan are now being made the guilty parties instead of the criminals who killed them, while the killers roam free to commit other hate crimes. Jesus Christ, in agony on the cross to which he was nailed, could pray: 'Father, forgive them for they know not what they do.' But the Hindus among us cannot utter a similar prayer because those who kill and maim and terrify in the name of Hinduism know exactly what they are doing and take pride in doing it. Such things have happened in all countries and centuries when religious fanaticism or racism has been allowed to go unchecked, and more especially when a ruling ideology gives free rein to fanaticism.

Then there is the political reason. Hindutva is a political invention that has redefined Hinduism for its political purpose, which is to declare India a Hindu rashtra. It says this country is exclusively

Hindu, all other Indians being invaders and outsiders. Historically this is incorrect since, like every other land mass, and the civilization that has grown out of it, the India we live in is the outcome of migrations millennia ago. There is no 'pure' race on earth. We are all a mixture of all that has gone into the making of us. The invaders and outsiders from earliest times are as Indian as the first aborigine inhabitants of this land mass. Which came first, the chicken or the egg, doesn't matter. Here we are today, people of every known religion, language, culture and lifestyle, and all rightful citizens of India.

As this is a reality that Hindutva finds hard to digest, those whom it claims as its supporters deal with it in two ways: One, the straightforward military solution of eliminating those whom you see as Other, or those who do not fall in line with your ideology. It began with Mahatma Gandhi being shot dead for committing the blasphemy of declaring that God is One whom we call by different names, and for giving us the mantra 'Ishvar Allah tere nam; sab ko sanmat de Bhagvan'. We can now see his murder in 1948 as the forerunner of what is happening to diversity, debate and dissent in our own time.

The second solution is to do the same thing with the printed page, by wiping out all trace of the Other from history books and inventing a

Hindutva history in its place. We have been told that Akbar was not Great and that it was Maharana Pratap Singh who won the battle of Haldighati. But now the texts in some Hindutva-ruled states have apparently gone further and decided to wipe out the Mughal empire altogether. Perhaps their textbooks will go much further back a thousand years and wipe out the Muslim invasions because Hindutva holds that these invasions and conquests were an interruption of Hindu history which is the rightful history of India, so all the rest is irrelevant. This campaign to wipe out memory itself is essential to the project of mind control which seeks to make us a uniform think-alike breed. It is part of this campaign to discredit Gandhi's non-violence as a policy that emasculated Indians, and to reject compassion as a resort of weaklings. How could such a wrong interpretation be made when no greater courage has been shown than that of the unarmed Indians who faced the armed might of an empire, and when compassion is the most civilized achievement of the human mind? Bertrand Russell once called politics 'the grinning devil' and this is what politics under the rule of Hindutva seems to have become. Vast slices of our multi-religious, multi-cultural heritage—which includes our literature, architecture, language, food, music, dance, dress and manners—are being dishonoured and disowned, leaving us shrunk into a monoculture which is not only not Hinduism, but the antitheses of all that India has stood for, worked for, and safeguarded as a proud and cherished inheritance. Not least, it is what India has been acclaimed and admired for throughout the world, as a thriving example of unity in diversity.

In contrast, let us look at politics as it once was. It was Mahatma Gandhi, a deeply religious Hindu, who laid the foundation of modern India when he created a national movement that cut across all divisions of region, religion, caste, language and gender and, for the first time in any country's history, brought class and mass together under the same banner to fight for freedom. It was a largely Hindu constituent assembly consisting mostly of elderly conservative Hindus who rejected a religious identity at Independence and declared India a secular democratic republic for the very reason that it is a deeply religious country of many different religions—and made religion a private affair, converting this into a Constitutional guarantee that gave every citizen the right to worship as he or she chose. It was this republic of millions of devout believers of different faiths that repeatedly elected a prime minister who was a known agnostic, yet also known for his profound respect for the religious beliefs of his countrymen, and determined that every Indian should hold and practise his or her faith in freedom. This was India at its birth into nationhood seventy years ago and it has remained so—until now when the politics of Hindutva has partitioned our country a second time, dividing Indians into Hindus and Others.

It is no comfort to know that there is a world trend toward a militant nationalism, toward tightening identity into cubbyholes, toward excluding those whom it considers Other, toward an era of post-truth in which facts have no place and invention rules the day. As inheritors of a hard-built tradition of democracy and secularism, we must prove ourselves an exception to this trend.

Full text of Nayantara Sahgal's undelivered speech intended for the 92nd Akhil Bhartiya Marathi Sahitya Sammelan held at Yavatmal, January 2019. Sahgal was disinvited after local pressure on the event organizers.

This is an emotional moment for me and I feel privileged to be here with you. I feel I am standing in the shadow of great Maharashtrians—Mahadev Govind Ranade who founded this sammelan, and whose name is part of the modern history of our country, and the distinguished Marathi writers who have chaired its conventions, and all the writers who have taken part in its sessions and whose writing has enriched the great creative enterprise known as Indian literature.

It is also an emotional moment for me because of my own connection with Maharashtra through my father, Ranjit Sitaram Pandit. I would like to tell you a little about him. He was a Sanskrit scholar from a family of distinguished Sanskrit scholars and he translated three Sanskrit classics into English: *Mudra Rakshasa*, Kalidas's *Ritusamhara*, and *Rajtarangini*. *Rajtarangini* is the twelfth century history of the kings of Kashmir by Kalhana, and it had a special fascination for my father because his two great loves were Sanskrit and Kashmir. He worked on this translation during two of his jail terms under British rule, and dedicated it to his Kashmiri father-in-law, Pandit Motilal Nehru. His brother-in-law, Jawaharlal Nehru, wrote an introduction to this work when it was published. I am deeply grateful to Dr Aruna Dhere and Shri Prashant Talnikar for their great labour of translating this massive history into my father's, and their own, native tongue, Marathi. I know that nothing would have made him happier.

Both my parents took part in the national movement for freedom under Mahatma Gandhi. My mother, Vijaya Lakshmi Pandit, was imprisoned three times and my father four times. During his fourth imprisonment he fell seriously ill in the terrible conditions and environment of Bareilly jail, and was given no medical treatment and my mother was not informed how very ill he was. Yet he had refused to ask for his release. When she was finally informed of his condition she was allowed to have a twenty-minute interview with him. It took place, according to the rule, in the office of the jail superintendent and under his watchful eye, which gave a political prisoner no privacy with his visitor. It shocked my mother to see him brought in on a stretcher. His head had been shaved and his body was emaciated. She almost broke down at the sight of him but somehow she held back her tears because she knew he would not want her to cry in front of the jailer. He told her why he wouldn't ask for the favour of being released. He said, 'I have fought with the lions, Gandhi and Nehru. Do you want me to behave like a jackal now?' She knew she couldn't change his mind so she controlled herself and sat near the stretcher and held his hand, and gave him news of home and the children, and what was growing in the garden he loved. When the government released him at last, it was only to die about three weeks later. Many years later, after Independence, my mother was India's high commissioner in Britain, and sat next to Prime Minister Winston Churchill at a lunch, and he said to her, 'We killed your husband, didn't we?' It was an admission that took her by surprise.

Most of you were not born in the 1940s, and you grew up in an independent country, so I have shared this personal story with you to show you the courage and discipline of those times, and the spirit of the men and women who fought for freedom. My parents were among many thousands of Indians—known and unknown, young and old—who committed their lives to that great fight and suffered all kinds of hardship because they had a passion for freedom. I want to ask you, do we have that same passion for freedom today?

Are we worthy of those men and women who have gone before us, some of whom died fighting so that future Indians could live in freedom?

I am asking this question because our freedoms are in danger. The dangers to them are so much on my mind that when I was thinking about what I should say to you, I knew I had to talk about all that is happening in India today, because it is affecting every side of our lives: what we eat, whom we marry, what we think and what we write, and, of course, how we worship. Today we have a situation where diversity, and opposition to the ruling ideology, are under fierce attack. Diversity is the very meaning of our civilization. We have old literatures in many different languages. We eat different foods, we dress differently, we have different festivals, and we follow different religions.

Inclusiveness has been our way of life, and this ancient multi-cultural civilization whose name is India is a most remarkable achievement that no other country has known. Today it is threatened by a policy to wipe out our religious and cultural differences and force us into a single religious and cultural identity. At one stroke this policy wipes out the Constitutional rights of millions of our countrymen and women who are not Hindus, and makes invaders, outsiders and enemies of them. At Independence our founding fathers rejected a religious identity and had the wisdom to declare India a secular democratic republic, not because they were against religion but because they understood that in our deeply religious country of many religions, only a secular state would provide the overall umbrella of neutrality under which every Indian would have the right to live and worship according to his or her faith. The Constitutent Assembly which took this decision was made up of a majority of Hindus, yet they drew up a Constitution whose preamble affirmed a life of liberty, equality and fraternity for all Indians. This high ideal was inspired by Ambedkar, who was the chief architect of the Constitution, and a great Maharashtrian whose insistence that all human beings are equal, started a revolution against caste. That high ideal has now been thrown aside. The minorities, and those who don't support the Hindu rashtra agenda, have become targets for fanatics who roam the streets. We have recently seen five citizens falsely charged with conspiracy and arrested on grounds of sedition. These are men and women who have spent years of their lives working for tribal rights and forest rights, and for justice for the marginalized. Christian churches have been vandalized and Christians are feeling insecure. Lynch mobs are openly attacking and killing Muslims on invented rumours that they were killing cows and eating beef. We are watching all this lawlessness on TV. In Uttar Pradesh these mob attacks on the cow pretext have become common, while the authorities stand by and look on. When terrorism of this kind becomes official, as it has in Uttar Pradesh, where can we look for justice? Mob violence backed by the state goes on in many places on defenceless people, and the guilty have not been convicted. In some cases their victims have been charged with the crimes instead, and in some cases the criminals have been congratulated. The human cost of this tragic situation is that it is a time of fear and grief for many Indians who no longer feel safe living and worshipping as they have always done, and have a right to do. The poor and helpless among them—some of whom have been driven out of their villages and their homes and jobs—are living without work, or help, or hope, or future.

I write novels and my material for storytelling has been political. As we writers know, we do not choose our material. We make stories out of the material and atmosphere around us, and because I grew up during the years of the fight for freedom, the values of that time and of the nation it created have been the stuff of my fiction and non-fiction. I have thought of my novels as being about the making of modern India. But because my last two novels are about the times we are now living in, they are about the 'un-making' of modern India.

As we are writers, let us look at what is happening to our fellow writers and artists in this political atmosphere. We are seeing that the questioning mind, the creative imagination, and freedom of expression have no place in the present political climate, and where there is no respect for freedom of thought or for democratic rights, writing becomes a risky activity. This has always been the case in authoritarian regimes all over the world where art is kept under state control and writers face punishment and persecution if they step out of line. Take the example of a young poet called Josef Brodsky in Stalin's Soviet Union. Brodsky is arrested and his interrogator waves a paper at him and says, 'Do you call yourself a poet? Do you call this a poem? It is not a poem if it makes no material contribution to the Soviet Union.' And he throws Brodsky into jail. Years later, Josef Brodsky wins the Nobel

Prize for Literature. Another famous Russsian case is of Solzhenitsin, who was condemned to hard labour in Siberia for many years for criticizing the government, and who also won the Nobel Prize for Literature. And now the same ignorance about art and literature is in action here, and writers are facing the anger of ignorant criticism, and much worse. Three eminent Maharashtrian rationalists, Narendra Dabholkar, Govind Pansare, and M.M. Kalburgi, have been shot dead for rejecting superstition in favour of reason, and Gauri Lankesh of Bengaluru for her independent views and her opposition to Hindutva. Others have been threatened with death and forbidden to write. We are told, 'Don't publish your book or we will burn it. Don't exhibit your paintings or we will destroy your exhibition. Filmmakers are told, 'Change the dialogue in this scene and cut out the next scene or we will not let your film be shown, and if you show it we will attack the cinema hall. Don't do anything to hurt our sentiments.' In other words, they are saying: do as you are told, or your life and your art are not safe. But the creative imagination cannot take orders from the state, or from the mob. And the question of hurting sentiments is, of course, nonsense. A population of one billion people cannot be made to think alike. Every community has its own views and its own sensitivities on various issues. But sentiments cannot decide what is right or wrong. In some cases it is even our duty to hurt sentiments. If we had been forbidden to hurt sentiments, we would still be burning widows, and no reform of any kind would have taken place. Many sentiments were hurt when the Hindu Code Bill was being debated and sadhus threw stones at Parliament House. But if the Bill had not been passed, Hindu women would have had no rights.

Historians are feeling the heat now that Indian history has been brought under state control. In some states large chunks of the past have been distorted or done away with altogether. And this is the work of Hindutva minds who have been specially chosen to rewrite it. If I were to invent a dialogue between an Indian historian and one of these rewriters of Indian history, it would go something like this. The historian says to the rewriter: 'Akbar won the battle of Haldighati. But in this book you are saying that he lost it. How come?' The rewriter replies, 'He lost it because I have decided that he lost it. History is what we say it is.'

Some of these rewritten textbooks have wiped out the whole Mughal empire, and not content with wiping out the past, all remaining reminders of it are being demolished. The Babri Masjid has been knocked down, and Mughal and Muslim names of towns and roads are being changed. Some textbooks have censored all mention of Nehru, whose governments laid the foundation of modern India, and Mahatma Gandhi was of course murdered by this mentality in 1948 for the blasphemy of the mantra he gave us: Ishvar Allah tere nam; Sab ko sammati de Bhagvan. Gandhi's non-violence is seen as emasculating Indians and making cowards of them. Personally I think that nothing needed greater heroism than the way unarmed Indians confronted the armed might of an empire. One of my novels called *Lesser Breeds* is my tribute to that unique time.

With all that is being wiped out, so is the scientific frame of mind that we have cultivated since Independence. It is being replaced by myths and legends, and a medieval frame of mind.

We have been justly proud of the key institutions we have built up since Independence, but they, too, have been brought under state control—whether they concern art and literature, or history, or technology, or science, information, education and culture. Our public universities, our museums and Akademies are no longer independent institutions. The Nehru Memorial Museum and Library in Delhi was an early example of the damage that is being done to our institutions, and Jawaharlal Nehru

University is an ongoing target of Hindutva hatred. As a Hindu and a believer in the great enlightened inheritance known as sanatan dharma, I cannot accept Hindutva.

In this war that has been declared on diversity, dissent and debate, those who care about freedom have not stayed silent. There are marches and rallies against the destruction of our fundamental rights. There are protests by retired civil servants, by students and academics, lawyers, historians and scientists, Dalits and Adivasis, and the farmers' huge demand for their rights. The Bhim Army, named after Dr Ambedkar, is making its voice heard, and we are reminded that it has an inheritance of dramatic revolt, when Ambedkar and E.V. Ramasamy Periyar publicly burned the Manusmriti in the 1920s for the insulting and objectionable laws it laid down for Dalits in the caste system, condemning them to an inferior status. The singer, T.M. Krishna, and the historian, Ramchandra Guha, are among those who have made strong individual protests. Krishna's concert was cancelled and Ram Guha received a death threat. Recently a great actor, Naseeruddin Shah, has spoken out against the war on Islam and how he fears for his children.

What can writers do in this situation? The answer is: we can write. Powerful fiction has been the result of writers stepping into controversy and taking sides, but not as polemics or propaganda. Their plays and poems and novels have been about people, not ideas, and they have been written by authors who were deeply engaged with the times they were living in, and some are still living in. Writers don't live in ivory towers.

Through our writing we take sides between good and evil, right and wrong. Great literature worldwide by writers of many nationalities has done this, and this is the literature that has touched chords in succeeding generations, and stays alive. We show where we stand by the subjects we choose, the stories we write, and the way we write them. Whether we are writing about our grandmother's cooking, or the rain on the roof, or describing the body of our beloved, every word we write makes it clear where we stand. Writing, like all forms of creative art, is a powerful form of political activism, and it is a means of revolt. That is why dictators are so afraid of it and take steps to control it.

A writers' protest started as an Award Wapsi movement three years ago, when about a hundred of us returned our Sahitya Akademi awards over the murder of an award-winning writer, Dr Dabholkar, which the Akademi took no notice of. But after the lynching of the poor blacksmith, Mohammed

Akhlaq, in Dadri village outside Delhi, our movement has grown and widened to cover other issues concerning attacks on democracy and human rights.

I have mentioned the writing of foreign writers. It has left its mark on my mind because I have been able to read some of it in translation. What about Indian writing in our many languages? It is a tragedy that we cannot read each other for lack of translation. Though our music and dance and theatre and films bring us together, our literatures keep us apart, and we cannot know each other until we can read each other. I can only hope that publishers will fill this gap, and that Indian literatures will become available not only to us but across the world.

I have to pay a special tribute to Maharashtrian women writers, because of the formidable obstacles that women have to overcome when they put their life experiences into words on a page. They run the risk of offending husband, family, and society, and suffering the consequences. May their courage and their creative energy go from strength to strength.

I want to thank my hosts for giving me this opportunity to speak to you, and I have spoken from the heart because of the crossroads our country is at. Which way we go—towards freedom or away from it—will depend, among other things, on what we write, and our refusal to be bullied into silence. In memory of the Indians who have been murdered, in support of all those who are upholding the right to dissent, and of the dissenters who live in fear and uncertainty, but still speak their minds, let us choose freedom.

Thank you for listening to me.

Kiran Nagarkar's open letter to Prime Minister Narendra Modi, published in Scroll.in, *29 March 2016*

Why is there such a gap between your wonderful words and your actions?

Dear Prime Minister Modiji,

On March 17, you outdid yourself on the first day of the World Sufi Forum hosted in Delhi. What could one say except, 'What a speech, how moving.' You had done your homework and you obviously have total recall (it would also be interesting to find out who your speechwriters are) but the fact remains that you are able to reproduce their amalgam of fact and rhetoric into an extempore mix.

This is what you said:

'Welcome to a land that is a timeless fountain of peace, and an ancient source of traditions and faiths, which has received and nurtured religions from the world. Welcome to a people with an abiding belief in Vasudhaiva Kutumbakam, the world is one family.'

Let me not resent the liberties you took with our past but pass it off as your version of Indian history. The list of the saints you name and quote is like a Who's Who in not just the Indian Sufi world but the whole international Sufi heritage—the Persian poet-philosopher Sadi, and Delhi's own Mehboob-eh-Ilahi, Hazarat Bakhtiyar Kaki and Hazrat Nizamuddin Aulia. You also referred to Khwaja Moinuddin Chishti, Bulleh Shah, Baba Farid, Amir Khusrau, Maulana Hussain Madani, Jalaluddin Rumi, Guru Nanak, Buddha, the Guru Granth Sahib, Mahavir, and Mahatma Gandhi. And you ended with the timeless prayer 'Om shanti, shanti, shanti.'

You had some genuinely wise things to say, like: 'We must reject any link between terrorism and religion. Those who spread terror in the name of religion are anti-religious.'

What noble sentiments. Now here's a prime minister that I felt we could all be proud of. And yet there was this low whisper telling me again and again something that the British Underground, along with the local train stations in Mumbai, have told us for years—mind the gap, mind the gap, mind the gap. That is the gap between the trains and the platforms where so many fall and are injured or die. In your case, Prime Minister, it's the credibility gap—the chasm between your wonderful words and zero action.

Let me quote your very words:

'...It is through openness and enquiry, engagement and accommodation, and respect for diversity that humanity advances, nations progress and the world prospers.'

What sane words. You remind me of Bhishma Pitamah from the *Mahabharata* at such times. You speak as wisely as the noble son of Shantanu. And just like him, when it's time to take a stand and back your words with concrete action, you retreat into silence and let the other leaders do the dirty work and take the blame. Or even worse, you pretend what is happening has nothing to do with you. You will recall that just a day after you spoke at the World Sufi Forum, your minister of state for human resource development, Ram Shankar Katheria, addressed a crowd of 5,000 in Agra. *The Times of India* reported that Katheria had demanded the withdrawal of hate speech cases against BJP and VHP leaders in Agra. 'If these cases are not withdrawn within the assured time, then Agra would witness a different Holi,' Katheria was quoted as saying. If this is the minister for education, the good Lord may not be able to help the students of Jawaharlal Nehru University or any other university.

The minister was referring to arrests made after several Bharatiya Janata Party and Vishwa Hindu Parishad leaders, including Katheria, made inflammatory speeches at a condolence meeting of a Vishwa Hindu Parishad worker in Agra in February. The worker was murdered, allegedly by a Muslim. At the condolence meeting, the BJP and VHP leaders equated Muslims with demons. VHP's district secretary Ashok Lavania called for murder. 'Revenge for the killing of one brother, demands the killing of ten rakshas,' he said. After protests following the hate speeches, FIRs were finally lodged against BJP leader and corporator Kundanika Sharma and three others. There was none against Katheria since, like his seniors, he claimed he never said anything against the Muslims. It is these cases that Katheria now wants withdrawn.

The American effect

Have you heard *Strange Fruit*, a song that Billie Holiday, perhaps the most famous black jazz singer from the United States, sang? And each time she did, she broke down. I must confess I had no idea what she was talking about for the longest time.

Here are the lyrics of *Strange Fruit*, Prime Minister:

Southern trees bear a strange fruit,
Blood on the leaves and blood at the root,
Black bodies swinging in the southern breeze,
Strange fruit hanging from the poplar trees.
Pastoral scene of the gallant south,
The bulging eyes and the twisted mouth,
Scent of magnolias, sweet and fresh,
Then the sudden smell of burning flesh.
Here is fruit for the crows to pluck,
For the rain to gather, for the wind to suck,
For the sun to rot, for the trees to drop,
Here is a strange and bitter crop.

She was of course singing a dirge for all those black victims of lynchings by white supremacists. Oddly enough, we who are so fond of emulating the American way of life—that country's fixation with free markets and the one per cent who earn far more than what at least fifty per cent of the population does—seem to have now decided to copy some of the worst American values when it comes to our minorities.

As you are well aware, earlier this month in Jharkhand, Mohammmad Majloom, 35, and Inayatullah Khan, 12, were gagged, their hands and legs tied and they were hung from a tree after being beaten with sticks and strangled.

Majloom was a trader escorting a few cattle to the market with the son of another cattle trader. The police think that the duo were murdered because the culprits wanted to steal their cattle. But they are also investigating the connection that one of the killers had with the Gau Raksha Samiti. If theft was the only reason, then one can—by a far-fetched stretch of the imagination—understand the murders. But the manner in which the man and boy were gagged, their bodies strapped and strung on the trees suggests a vile and violent hatred of the two.

Is it possible to talk to you, Modiji? After all you are not the Prime Minister of just the Rashtriya Swayamsevak Sangh, the Bharatiya Janata Party and its affiliates but of all the people of India. These people elected your party to power. We may not see eye-to-eye on some matters, a few of them very sensitive and crucial, but that's all the more reason for us to sit down and have a conversation instead of a one-way *Mann ki baat*, or your preferred see-no-evil, hear-no-evil, speak-no-evil stance.

Where does this violence come from? Not just the bloodthirsty violence in Muzaffarnagar, Dadri and other places but the violence in speech? Why this insecurity when you won fair and square with an overwhelming majority? Why this continuous victim-syndrome as Pratap Bhanu Mehta pointed out recently—whether it's the finance minister, Arun Jaitley, accusing Sahitya Akademi's award-winning authors of 'manufacturing protests' for returning their awards or your human resources development minister Smriti Irani insisting that the Jawaharlal Nehru University students were guilty of sedition even when she knew very well that the video footage had been doctored? What was the need for Rajnath Singh to retweet a fake Twitter handle that suggested that Pakistan-based Lashkar-e-Taiba chief Hafiz Saeed had supported the so-called seditious events at JNU in February?

Why this demand for every Indian to prove his or her loyalty to our country by saying Bharat Mata ki Jai? I'm sure, Prime Minister, you don't want to hear these words spoken by all those who have defrauded our country of thousands of crores, or have stabbed it in the back, and yet have the gall to swear their loyalty to Bharat Mata. Why fear the freedom of thought encouraged by the best universities? Why must those who don't fall in line with the tenets and theology of the ruling party be demonised? One thing that has bothered me for a long time (and let me clarify quickly that it has nothing to do with you) is a legacy of the previous government in Maharashtra. Perhaps you can help us in this matter. Here in Maharashtra, the national anthem is sung before every film shown in the theatres. Often, this happens before the audience is about to watch some dreadful Hollywood blockbluster like *Deadpool* or a mindless Bollywood song-and-dance extravaganza. If this is not a travesty of our anthem, I don't know what is. Along with the rest of the country I sang *Jana Gana Mana* full-throated for the first time on the two most important days in our nation's history—on 15 August 1947, and on 26 January 1950. Let us honour our flag and our national anthem and not invoke them so meaninglessly as if we do not understand the significance and the history of our unique non-violent freedom struggle.

Surely we can talk about these points without getting defensive or seeing some devious traitorous intent behind these questions.

But let me come to an issue that has been on my mind, and that I have wanted to share with you for several months. Let me repeat an old adage you may be familiar with: every action has a reaction. So far the Bharatiya Janata Party, the Vishwa Hindu Parishad, the Bajrang Dal, the Rashtriya Swayamsevak Sangh and many of its other incarnations have initiated various schemes to harass and victimise minority communities like the Muslims and Christians through their love jihad, ghar wapsi, bahu lao, beti bachao tactics.

It is these Hindutva groups that helped fan a frenzy around the slaughter of cows and eating beef, often in states where the slaughter of cows and consumption of beef had already been banned. Sometimes, this hysteria has tragic consequences. Last year, the farm labourer, Mohammad Akhlaq, in Dadri near Delhi, was falsely accused of having beef in his fridge. He and his youngest son were beaten with bricks by a Hindu mob. Akhlaq succumbed to the murderous attack while his son was critically injured. The Bharatiya Janata Party-led government in Maharashtra also banned the sale of old cattle with the result that the already beleaguered Indian farming community was driven further into penury and often to suicide.

How come, Dear Prime Minister, you have not read the riot act to your Islamophobic ministers, legislators, parliamentarians or the rest of the Parivar even once since you came to power? Some folks believe that it is because of these tirades and hate-filled actions that the BJP did not win the Delhi and Bihar elections, and predict that the elections in the four or five states due in the coming months will not be a walkover. I am no oracle but I know one thing for sure, your voter base is very strong.

Modiji, you are an astute politician and statesman. Can you not see that actions as well as the lack of action have consequences especially in these dark times? Surely you are familiar with the proverb 'as you sow, so shall you reap'. As I said earlier even silence has consequences. I cannot and will not believe that you want to alienate our Muslim brothers and sisters across the subcontinent and make the country one of the best recruiting centres for the Islamic State. So why have you not stopped this persecution of our own Muslim citizens?

I have heard many experts opine on television that our intelligence agencies are doing a fine job of keeping track of those Muslims who wish to join the Islamic State. I am glad to hear that but complacency would be a prescription for disaster. I have also heard them say authoritatively that our Muslim community will never really join the Islamic State in any substantial numbers. That is a marvellously myopic statement. As we have seen time and again, including the 26/11 attacks on Mumbai and the latest attack in Brussels, you don't need large numbers, you need just three to seven efficient and focused operatives to execute a deadly attack. Secondly, anyone with a little common sense will tell us that no community however small will have infinite patience and forbearance if continually provoked and prodded, and made to live in tension and fear. No, there will come a point when it will feel it has nothing to lose and strike back.

But here is the crux of the matter. Why in God's name and in the name of our Constitution are we so hell-bent on offending a huge chunk of India's own citizenry? The most important principle of secularism is to take everybody along. Muslims, like Dalits, have had a rough deal long enough. We have to open the doors to state-of-the-art education for them and make sure that they find suitable employment. It is our responsibility to erase the ignorance and superstition that Kabir and the other bhakti saints saw as the root cause of all our ills. We must welcome an open wide-as-the-sky mindset so that no Indian is left behind.

Come, Prime Minister Modiji, live up to your own words and show us the way to be together whatever our different faiths, agnosticism or atheism.

Yours truly,
Kiran Nagarkar

Kiran Nagarkar's open letter to Arun Jaitley, Minister of Finance and Corporate Affairs, published in Scroll.in, *9 March 2017*

Why do students get jailed but RSS leaders who issue vile threats walk freely?

Dear Mr Arun Jaitley,

Pranam, greetings, As-Salaam-Alaikum. I trust you are well and as usual, fighting fit.

As a lawyer you know better than most denizens of this country that the breath and heartbeat of democracy are openness, dissent, civility and non-violence. One other quality that Gandhi had in plenty, but is sorely missing these days, is a sense of humour about our follies. It ensures that we are not only self-aware but are able to internalise the notion that it is the bonds of brotherhood that are the foundation of this marvellous potpourri called India. It is in the light of this background that I find it incomprehensible and disturbing that a seasoned lawyer like you, who is also our finance minister, keeps talking about the imminent dangers to the polity just because a university student spoke openly about her desire to defend the right to freedom of expression and drew a fine but thoughtful line between the people of Pakistan and war.

A few weeks ago, I had written an article asking how we don't know who the enemy in the North-west is even after decades of being victimised. The enemy is definitely not the majority of Pakistanis who, like us Indians, are busy making ends meet. The enemy is the Pakistani Army and the Inter-Services Intelligence who control not just the terrorist organisations in Pakistan like the Taliban, Lashkar-e-Taiba, Al-Qaeda and Jaish-e-Mohammed, but also mastermind the planning and execution of terror attacks in India, and even in Pakistan itself, destroying the holy sites of Sufi saints and killing hundreds of their own people. We know that the Pakistani Army and the Inter-Services Intelligence control that country's prime minister himself and dictate policy. General Pervez Musharraf, the former Pakistan President, was happy to admit to this just a few days ago.

Who should know this better than you? After all you and Amit Shah are one of the triumvirate headed by Prime Minister Narendra Modi. We know that while your portfolio is finance, you often speak on behalf of Modiji and the Bharatiya Janata Party. You express your wrath often on every conceivable subject, especially the country's territorial integrity and the student community. But starting with your daily reversals and revisions in diktats during the demonetisation tsunami, why does almost everything have to boil down to a mantra of nationalism and patriotism? Why are you constantly fuming and conjuring up sedition fantasies? Why are you suffering from so much insecurity? Do you really believe that our beautiful, strong and ancient country, which weathered 250 years of foreign rule and many other disasters, is so shaky that it is in perpetual danger from a few students who express dissatisfaction with the state of the nation?

Come on Jaitleyji, you too were a firebrand in your youth with perhaps a different bee in your bonnet. India is unlike any other country. We have deep roots that go back all the way to Mahavir and the Buddha and to Gopal Krishna Gokhale, Rabindranath Tagore, Gandhiji, his colleagues and the foot-soldiers of our freedom struggle. Surely you and your party do not need to be reminded that this is how we are still the only country in the world that stood up to the might of the British Empire and won independence with the most unique weapon on earth, non-violent civil disobedience.

On the other hand, not for a moment do I underestimate the appalling danger that ISIS [Islamic State of Iraq and the Levant] poses to the free world. But there is a cure for ISIS. It is democracy at its best where every citizen has the same rights, the same superb education (not doctored texts by ideologues of any variety), the same opportunities and the same rights and duties. In short, a binding inclusiveness where everyone has an intense feeling of belonging to this land.

I hope to God that the citizens of our country will never permit the highly inflammable and barren hate campaigns of Donald Trump in the US, Marine Le Pen in France, Nigel Farage in the UK and so many others to find fertile ground in India.

Jaitleyji, if you want to win over the minds of youngsters, then 'chill out', as they put it, and sit amongst them minus your overheated rhetoric. Instead of talking down to them, talk with them about their ambitions, literature, idealism, the intense need for a wide-open and enlightened educational system, listen to their opinions. You will be amazed at how knowledgeable many of them are. Show them that the oxygen of democracy is freedom of expression and inclusiveness. Show them that you would have cared deeply about Gurmehar Kaur even if her father had not been a military man who lost his life. Show them that you would protect anyone—young women or men, the elderly or the middle-aged—because that is where this country's honour lies. That anybody who threatens a woman with rape, verbal or physical harm will be arraigned instantly and punished under the law. The same will hold for the threat of violence against anyone. And if it is not too much to ask, put an end to the glib doublespeak. Cut out the platitudes. Mean what you say. Insist on actual action, and show the people that our democracy is in top shape and functions for every single person.

As a highly-respected lawyer, perhaps you and Ravi Shankar Prasad, our minister of law, should remember that the only sacred—but non-religious—text in our polity is the Constitution of India. Forgive me for putting the matter in such a tentative manner but the two of you and even our much-revered prime minister often have memory lapses and seem to be unaware of a document of such enormous importance. We must, however, grant that every now and then your memory is active enough to invoke the Constitution. For instance, we watched you flare up last year on the issue of Jawaharlal Nehru University's Kanhaiya Kumar, who was jailed on the charge of sedition, or regarding Rohith Vemula, the doctoral student from Hyderabad Central University who committed suicide after he was thrown out of his hostel room. In Vemula's case the government asked his mother to prove her Dalit antecedents within fifteen days. Are we to understand that the Dalit label has overnight become so highly prized that Vemula and his mother would claim to belong to the much-maligned 'wretched of the earth', as the psychoanalyst and philosopher Frantz Fanon called the poor and depressed classes?

Here's another instance. How could one forget that Mohammed Akhlaq of Dadri village in Uttar Pradesh was lynched by a mob, and his young son brutalized, because a Brahmin priest from the village temple claimed that there was beef in the family fridge? Police investigations and the forensic probe proved that there was no beef in the house. But months later, it turns out that the tested substance had changed its chemical or other components and gone back to being beef. So now Akhlaq's bereaved family is once again in serious trouble with the law.

How come you and Ravi Shankar Prasadji are so incensed when students voice their opinions that you hold forth on the danger to the nation from these young people, but seem utterly indifferent to the law transmuting Akhlaq's victimised family into criminals? It is incomprehensible how the government can alienate our minority communities with such abandon.

And here's one more egregious case of antagonising our own people. I am talking about what happened in Kashmir a few months ago. Let us grant that things got out of hand. Was that so unusual? Our relationship with that former jannat (paradise) has been dicey from the time we won independence. Could you two senior ministers at the Centre, the honorable prime minister, the home minister and the chief of the army not see the horrendous consequences of firing pellets that blinded so many people, especially children? How have we become so callous and blind? Surely there are many other less dangerous but effective methods of controlling mobs. Can't you see that you are not just making lifelong enemies, you are ensuring that the next fifty or hundred generations will keep these terrible crimes and injustices alive, and never forgive us? Can you not see that the Indian State is turning into the most efficient recruiting agency for ISIS in India?

Then on March 2, Kundan Chandravat, a Rashtriya Swayamsevak Sangh pracharak pramukh (joint head of dissemination for RSS ideology) announced a one-crore bounty for anyone who murdered Pinarayi Vijayan, the chief minister of Kerala. According to Chandravat, Vijayan was responsible for the deaths of 300 RSS activists in the state. Were these alleged murders a clandestine operation by chief minister Vijayan that even the Centre was unaware of, or was this just routine Rashtriya Swayamsevak Sangh political hyperbole? But Chandravat had more poison to share with the public. He said he was willing to 'offer a garland of 300,000 human skulls to Bharatmata in revenge'.

As expected, the RSS leadership announced that it was disassociating the institution from this statement and its source. However, there was total silence from the Union government. Modiji, Jaitleyji, Prasadji, and Singhji, there was not a peep out of you. When it comes to India's youngsters, you hector people, you spew extreme disapproval and your diatribes get louder and more intolerant and more hostile, all in the name of sedition. But you take zero note and action when someone from the RSS, in full public view, using the most obnoxious words, threatens death to a chief minister and three lakh citizens. Is silence all you can offer to such vile threats? While students get jailed, Chandravat gets to walk freely and spread his deadly talk without the police or the leadership of the ruling party doing a thing.

So, does our country now have two Constitutions—one for the ruling party and its affiliates, and another for the rest of the country? This also raises another question: why has the judiciary not issued a suo moto notice to Chandravat yet?

I will take my leave now. Do remember that there is no malice here, just what the French call 'a cry from the heart'.

Warm regards, and may God keep all of you safe and in good health,

Kiran Nagarkar

PS: One simple question: How come we, the people of this land, cannot have a conversation with you, Prime Minister Modi, Amit Shah, Ravi Shankar Prasad, and most of your leaders and spokespersons? The slightest disagreement and all of you come down on us as if we were traitors. Is it not possible to lower the temperature and talk to each other instead of being constantly slammed down? Is dialogue with all of us outside the pale of Hindutva? It might come as a shock to you but we are not the enemy. We too belong to the same country as you and are Indians.

Epilogue: On Grief

Gita Sahgal

The essence of my relationship with Kiran was our sensitivity to each other's state of mind and being. He had shared my anguish over my beloved grandson Ayan's long struggle with mental illness and compares it, in an email, with his own 'nightmare' of suffering through illness in his childhood. He had met Gita and Ayan at a litfest I was taking part in, in Chandigarh, and felt deeply involved with what they were going through. Later his support meant much to me through my breakdown at Ayan's death. Hence I have included here Gita's effort to assuage her grief, and below it, a poem I had shown Kiran, written by Ayan at the tender age of thirteen.—Nayantara Sahgal

Message to Muswell Hill volunteers, guests and workers at the shelter:

My name is Gita. I have many friends who are cooks, who cook for a living, or who cook as volunteers in various community centres, migrant centres, and other places. I have only ever cooked at home, for family and friends. Today for the first time I cooked a meal for people I didn't know. It was like a blessing to me at this time of fear and sorrow, and in my total isolation, to be able to do it.

Last year my son Ayan (nicknamed Zum) aged twenty-three, died in very tragic circumstances. He had suffered from severe mental health issues and was living in accommodation paid for by the National Health Service. He was failed by the system in many ways but he was always conscious that there were people who were far worse off than him, people who should have had support and decent housing but were given nothing. Whatever he had, he shared. He made friends with people on the street and people he had known in hospital, many of whom had no family or friends to support them.

Ayan often felt lonely, but he had friends whom he had known since he was at school. One of these was Arthur who is now a chef and cooked for you today as well. Arthur had known Ayan since they were both boys, when they dreamed and fought and got into trouble together. Last year Arthur had to do what no young person should have to do. He delivered a eulogy for Ayan at his funeral.

Since then, Ayan's young friends and I have

worked together to find ways of honouring his memory and that of other people who are vulnerable. Ayan's friends raised money for a music charity, Nordoff Robbins, and money for a bench with a memorial plaque in his memory in the grounds of a park, Alexandra Palace, where they had played as children and hung out as teenagers. The plaque read:

Our beloved Zum
You are always in our thoughts,
Somewhere for a lost soul to sit,
In memory of Ayan Joshi
1996-2019

We also made a short video about the threat to the NHS, the dangers of privatized services and the rise in male suicides. We will continue to highlight issues we think are important. It is one way of dealing with grief.

Another way is to cook. I am so grateful to be able to cook for others and not simply for myself. I would like to continue to do it. Please let me know what you would like to eat and I will try and make it. It is the greatest balm for grief that I know.

Below: The poem I had shown Kiran, written by Ayan at the age of thirteen for a school project, which reveals his painful awareness of the times he was living in.

Identical Forces

Fighting, never stopping, until they've won the
battle,
Filled with hatred and prejudice without any
reason,
Maybe peer pressure, maybe the way they grew up,
Born loathing the other side, which is identical,

Racism that fills their blood for the enemy
And love that fills their heart for their fellow
fighters.
'Grenades, Molotovs, what else can we throw
into the mosque?'

'Grenades, Molotovs, what else can we throw
into the temple?'
'Fear, what is fear? Fear of dying? Nonsense.
You don't fear what will bring you great
martyrdom,
And why shall you fear the pain that only lasts a
moment,
When straight after you will be happy forever'.
Crazy, not for one moment considering their
reasons,
Thinking only of the destruction of their enemy.
The only reason that even makes sense to fight is
revenge:
'You killed my father!'
'You killed my brother!'
Now they are even, or are they ever?

Notes

1. Nayantara Sahgal's memoir, first published in 1954, reprinted by HarperCollins India, 2007.
2. Pandit Jawaharlal Nehru, India's first prime minister and brother of Sahgal's mother, Vijayalakshmi Pandit.
3. *Nehru's India: Essays on the Maker of a Nation*, pub. Speaking Tiger, 2015.
4. Tulsi Vatsal, Kiran Nagarkar's wife and author of several books.
5. Novel by Nayantara Sahgal, pub. HarperCollins India, 2000.
6. Book launch of *Nehru's India: Essays on the Maker of a Nation*, on 5 August 2015 at the Nehru Memorial Library, Delhi.
7. Launch of *Nehru's India* on 5 August 2015, at Nehru Memorial Library, New Delhi.
8. Benjamin Netanyahu, prime minister of Israel between 1996-1999 and 2009-2021, and currently leader of the opposition.
9. Arun Jaitley, Supreme Court lawyer and politician, who served as the minister for finance and corporate affairs in the BJP government from 2014-2019. Jaitley passed away in August 2019.
10. *Nehru's India: Essays on the Maker of a Nation.*
11. The murders of the writers M.M. Kalburgi, Narendra Dabholkar and Govind Pansare by Hindu fundamentalists,

after which Sahgal returned her award to the Sahitya Akademi in October 2015.

12. Lawyer, researcher and human rights activist based in New Delhi.
13. Academic, novelist and literary critic, formerly professor of English at Jawaharlal Nehru University, Dehi, and director of the Indian Institute of Advanced Study, Shimla, since 2018.
14. Writer and author of several novels and short stories.
15. A cultural and academic community of writers, thinkers, activists and artists, founded by Githa Hariharan and, amongst others, poet K. Satchinandan, and historian Romila Thapar.
16. Former president of Jawaharlal Nehru University Students' Union and national leader of the All India Students Federation, now a member of the Communist Party of India. In February 2016, Kumar was arrested by the Delhi Police on charges of sedition at a rally on the JNU campus held to commemorate the second anniversary of the hanging of the Parliament attack convict Afzal Guru. He was released on bail in March 2016.
17. The Hay Festival of Literature and Arts held at Hay-on-Wye in the UK.
18. George W. Bush served as the 43rd president of the United States from 2001-2009; Richard Bruce Cheney served as Bush's vice-president; Donald Rumsfield served as the US Secretary of Defence from 1975 to 1977 under President Gerald Ford and again from 2001-2006 under Bush.
19. Barrack Obama, who served as the 44th US president from 2009-2017.
20. Former vice president of Development Economics and chief economist of the World Bank, senior US Treasury Department official throughout President Bill Clinton's administration, and former director of the National Economic Council for President Obama.

21. Ruchir Joshi, writer, filmmaker and columnist was the long-time partner of Sahgal's daughter, Gita, which whom he had two sons, Zum and Kabir.
22. Nayantara Sahgal was presented with the Lal Dedh National Award in September 2018. Instituted by Sarhad, a Pune-based social, cultural and educational organisation which is dedicated to the cause of helping the people of strife-torn border regions, the award is named after Lalleshwari or 'Lal Ded', a 14th-century mystic saint-poetess from the Kashmir valley known for her own style of mystic poetry called 'vakhs' which still remains an important part of modern Kashmiri literature.
23. A reference to the court case filed against Sahgal by relatives, laying claim to her house in Dehradun where she has lived for the past thirty years.
24. Nonika Sahgal, Sahgal's elder daughter.
25. The #MeToo movement was founded by Tarana Burke in the US in 2006 against sexual abuse and harassment perpetrated by powerful men in society but began as a social phenomenon in October 2017 as a hashtag started by American actress Alyssa Milano who shared her story of sexual assault by film producer Harvey Weinstein. In October 2018, the movement reached India's mainstream public discourse. A number of women came out with allegations and accounts of harassment on social media and other platforms.
26. In April 2019, Nayantara Sahgal became the first recipient of the Loknete Bhai Vaidya Smruti Gaurav Puraskar, set up in memory of the socialist leader, Bhai Vaidya, who was home minister of Maharashtra in 1978. He was also responsible for reviving the Socialist Party of India and continued to be its president till the last few years before his death in 2018.
27. Vinayak Damodar 'Veer' Savarkar was a politician, activist,

and writer. He developed the Hindu nationalist political ideology of Hindutva while imprisoned at Ratnagiri in 1922. He was a leading figure in the Indian independence movement and the Hindu Mahasabha; Madhavrao Sadashivrao Golwalkar was the second Sarsanghchalak of the Rashtriya Swayamsevak Sangh (RSS). He has been widely noted to be the most prominent ideologue of Hindutva; Nathuram Godse, also a member of the RSS, was the assassin of Mahatma Gandhi, whom he shot dead in New Delhi on 30 January 1948.

ALSO BY NAYANTARA SAHGAL IN SPEAKING TIGER

NEHRU'S INDIA

ESSAYS ON THE MAKER OF A NATION

SPEAKING TIGER

Edited and with an Introduction by:

Nayantara Sahgal

Insightful and thought-provoking essays by some of our foremost writers and thinkers that examine Nehru's legacy and its continuing relevance in 21st century India.

Category: Anthology/Non-Fiction
Binding: Hardback
Extent: 192 pp
Imprint: Speaking Tiger
Territory: World
Pub: July 2015
ISBN: 978-93-85288-26-5
Price: ₹ 399

THE BOOK

For much of the country's post-Independence history, Indian politics was dominated by a single towering figure: Jawaharlal Nehru. A leading figure of the Independence movement, and Mahatma Gandhi's chosen successor, Nehru, as India's first prime minister, from 1947 until his death in 1964, was the architect of its birth as a modern nation-state: a sovereign, socialist, secular and democratic republic.

In this volume, some of our foremost thinkers and writers examine the different aspects of Nehru's personality and his legacy.

Nehru's influence stretched beyond the Freedom Movement and the political and bureaucratic boundaries of prime ministerhood. A man of letters, it was Nehru who initiated the setting up of the Sahitya Akademi devoted to literature, the National School of Drama and the National Institute of Design; just as, in the field of technology and business management, he established the Indian Institutes of Technology and the Indian Institutes of Management across the country. He was equally the force behind the setting up of dams and factories, which he regarded as the temples of modern India.

ALSO BY NAYANTARA SAHGAL IN SPEAKING TIGER

SPEAKING TIGER

WHEN THE MOON SHINES BY DAY

Nayantara Sahgal

Category: Fiction
Format: B
Page Extent: 168 pages
Binding: Hardback
Territory: World
Pub: September 2017
ISBN: 978-93-86702-11-1
Price: ₹399

BISAC Category:
FICTION/Literary
FICTION/Political
FICTION/Dystopian
FICTION/Satire

'A riveting work of political voltage, dramatic vigour and deep human veracity from one of India's most sensitive writers.'

—Gopalkrishna Gandhi

Key Selling Points

- A powerful political novel from one of the most important voices of our times, Nayantara Sahgal.
- Though written as fiction, the novel paints a candid picture of present-day India, its politics and cultural transformation, and carries a significant message for the future, especially with regard to the Dalits and other minorities.
- The novel will appeal to those interested in politics as well as lovers of good literary fiction.
- Nayantara Sahgal is the author of more than twenty works of fiction and non-fiction, winner of the Sahitya Akademi Award, the Sinclair Prize and the Commonwealth Prize. She has an established readership and is one of the most respected writers of our times.

Description

India has changed. Rehana finds her father's books on medieval history have been 'disappeared' from bookstores and libraries. Her young domestic help, Abdul, discovers it is safer to be called Morari Lal in the street, but there is no such protection from vigilante fury for his Dalit friend, Suraj. Kamlesh, a diplomat and writer, comes up against official wrath for his anti-war views. A bomb goes off at Cyrus Batliwala's gallery on the opening day of an art show.

Presiding over this new world is the Director of Cultural Transformation, whose smiling affability masks a relentless agenda to create a Hindu master race.

In this atmosphere, Rehana and her three book-club friends, Nandini, Aruna and Lily, meet every week to discuss a book one of them has chosen—their oasis of peace amidst the harshness of reality—even as Rehana's German friend, Franz Rohner, haunted by his country's Nazi past, warns her of what is to come. All revolutions, he wryly observes, follow the same path. But is India about to prove him wrong?

In this brilliant, dystopian satire, Nayantara Sahgal draws a telling portrait of our times.

The Author

Nayantara Sahgal is the author of several works of fiction and non-fiction, the first of which, *Prison and Chocolate Cake*, an autobiography, was published in 1954. Her works include classic novels such as *Rich Like Us*, *Plans for Departure* and *Lesser Breeds*. She has received the Sahitya Akademi Award, the Sinclair Prize and the Commonwealth Writers' Prize. She is a Member of the American Academy of Arts & Sciences. She has been awarded the Diploma of Honour from the International Order of Volunteers of Peace (Italy), and an Honorary Doctorate of Letters from the University of Leeds. She returned her Akademi Award in 2015 in protest against the murder by vigilantes of three writers, and the Akademi's silence at the time. She has been a Vice President of the PUCL (People's Union for Civil Liberties) and is engaged in an ongoing protest against the assaults on the freedom of expression and democratic rights.

Praise

'Nayantara Sahgal is one of our most illuminating novelists, who has carefully and sensitively recorded for much of independent India's existence the impact of politics and ideology on individual lives.'—Pankaj Mishra

ALSO BY NAYANTARA SAHGAL IN SPEAKING TIGER

SPEAKING
TIGER

THE FATE OF BUTTERFLIES

Nayantara Sahgal

One of our most courageous and eloquent storytellers, Nayantara Sahgal's superb mastery over language and history make this bold new work a compelling story that is as disturbing as it is beautifully told.

Key Selling Points

- A powerful political novel from one of the most important voices of our times, Nayantara Sahgal
- Though written as fiction, the novel paints a candid picture of present-day India, its politics and cultural transformation, and carries a significant message for the future, especially with regard to Muslims and other minorities
- The novel will appeal to those interested in politics as well as lovers of good literary fiction
- Nayantara Sahgal is the author of more than twenty works of fiction and non-fiction, winner of the Sahitya Akademi Award, the Sinclair Prize and the Commonwealth Prize. Her novel, *When the Moon Shines by Day*, was longlisted for the 2018 JCB Prize
- She has an established readership and is one of the most respected writers of our times

Description

Prabhakar, returning home one evening, comes upon a corpse at a crossroads, naked but for the skullcap on his head. Days later, he listens to Katerina's stark retelling of a gang rape in a village, as chilling as only the account of a victim can be. And in a macabre sequence, he finds his favourite dhaba no longer serves gular kebabs and rumali roti, while Bonjour, the fine dining restaurant run by a gay couple, has been vandalised by goons.

Casting a long shadow over it all is Mirajkar, the 'Master Mind', brilliant policy maker and political theorist, who is determined to rid the country of all elements alien to its culture—as he, and his partymen, perceive it.

A professor of political science, Prabhakar observes these occurrences with deepening concern. Is the theory he put forth in his book—that it is not the influence of those who preach goodness and compassion that prevails, but the matter-of-factness of cruelty—playing out before him?

In the midst of all this, he meets Katerina, beautiful, half-Russian, wearing the scars of a brutal incident as a badge of honour. Together, they discover that, even in times that are grim, there is joy to be had.

The Author

Nayantara Sahgal is the author of several works of fiction and non-fiction, the first of which, *Prison and Chocolate Cake*, an autobiography, was published in 1954. Her works include classic novels such as *Rich Like Us, Plans for Departure* and *Lesser Breeds*. She has received the Sahitya Akademi Award, the Sinclair Prize and the Commonwealth Writers' Prize. Her novel, *When the Moon Shines by Day*, was longlisted for the 2018 JCB Prize. She returned her Akademi Award in 2015 in protest against the murder by vigilantes of three writers, and the Akademi's silence at the time. She has been a Vice President of the PUCL (People's Union for Civil Liberties) and is engaged in an ongoing protest against the assaults on the freedom of expression and democratic rights.

Praise

'In this breathtaking new novel, [Sahgal] confronts the toxic dangers of the historical moment—war, religious polarisation, authoritarian charisma, a dystopian future that is already upon us.'—Ranjit Hoskote

'*The Fate of Butterflies* is a brilliant, superbly told tale that is a meditation on what is happening in our country today. This brave and hugely readable novel is a telling comment on what may happen when a country's rulers try to wipe out chunks of its history and marginalize an entire community.'—Kiran Nagarkar

Category: Fiction
Format: B
Page Extent: 144 pp
Binding: Hardback
Publisher: Speaking Tiger
Territory: World
Pub: February 2019
ISBN: 978-93-88326-87-2
Price: ₹450

BISAC Categories:
FICTION/Literary
FICTION/Political